Tor is pr[...]
fiction's s[...]
particularly fine science fiction is written at
a length just too short to put in a book by
itself, so we're providing them two at a time.

The Tor Doubles will be both new stories and
older ones, all carefully chosen. Whichever
side you start with, you will be able to turn
the book over and enjoy the other side just
as much.

IMPRISONED UNDER THE RED SUN . . .
"But on Redsun you were betrayed?"
"I never expected them to use a child," Kylis
said bitterly.
"A child!"
"This little kid sneaked on my ship. He reminded me of me. He was only ten or eleven, and
he was all beat up. I guess we aren't so suspicious
of kids because most spaceport rats started at the
same age." Kylis glanced at Miria and saw that
she was staring at her, horrified.
"They used a child? And injured him, just to
catch you?"
"Does that really surprise you?"
"Yes," Miria said.
"Miria, half the people who were killed during
the last set weren't more than five or six years
older than the boy who turned me in. Most of the
people being sent here now are that age. What
could they possibly have done terrible enough to
get them sent here?"

The Tor Double Novels:

A Meeting with Medusa by Arthur C. Clarke/
Green Mars by Kim Stanley Robinson

Hardfought by Greg Bear/*Cascade Point* by
Timothy Zahn

Born with the Dead by Robert Silverberg/*The
Saliva Tree* by Brian W. Aldiss

Tango Charlie and Foxtrot Romeo by John
Varley/*The Star Pit* by Samuel R. Delany

No Truce with Kings by Poul Anderson/*Ship of
Shadows* by Fritz Leiber

Enemy Mine by Barry B. Longyear/*Another
Orphan* by John Kessel

Screwtop by Vonda N. McIntyre/*The Girl Who
Was Plugged In* by James Tiptree, Jr.

The Nemesis from Terra by Leigh Brackett/
Battle for the Stars by Edmond Hamilton

*forthcoming

VONDA N. McINTYRE

SCREWTOP

A TOM DOHERTY ASSOCIATES BOOK
NEW YORK

This is a work of fiction. All the characters and events portrayed in this book are fictitious, and any resemblance to real people or events is purely coincidental.

SCREWTOP

Copyright © 1976 by Vonda N. McIntyre

Reprinted by permission of the author and her agents, Marie Rodell–Frances Collin Literary Agency.

All rights reserved, including the right to reproduce this book or portions thereof in any form.

A TOR Book
Published by Tom Doherty Associates, Inc.
49 West 24 Street
New York, NY 10010

Cover art by Maren

ISBN: 0-812-54554-0   Can. ISBN: 0-812-55959-2

First Tor edition: April 1989

Printed in the United States of America

0 9 8 7 6 5 4 3 2 1

■ ■ ■

Hot and wet from the fine, steamy rain, Kylis sat on her heels at the top of the drilling pit and waited for the second-duty shift to end. She rubbed at a streak of the thick red mud that had spattered her legs and her white boots when she walked across the compound. Redsun's huge dim star altered colors; white became a sort of pinkish gray. But among the forest's black foliage and against the Pit's clay, white uniforms stood out and made prisoners easier for the guards to see.

A few other people waited with Kylis at the south end of the deep slash in the earth. Like them, she crouched unsheltered from the rain, strands of wet hair plastered to her cheeks, watching for friends she had not seen in forty days.

Below lay two completed generator domes; above them rose the immense delicate cooling towers, and the antenna beaming power along the relay system to North Continent.

Fences and guards protected the finished installations from the prisoners. Kylis and the rest worked only on clearing the fern forest, extending the Pit, drilling a third steam well—the dirty, dangerous jobs.

Paralleling the distant wall of volcanoes in the east, the drill pit extended northward. Its far end was invisible, obscured by the rain and by clouds of acrid smoke that billowed from the trash piles. The Pit was being lengthened again to follow the fault line where drilling was most efficient. Another strip of frond forest had been destroyed, and its huge primitive ferns now lay in blackened heaps. The stalks never burned completely, but until the coals died, a bank of irritating smoke and sticky ash would hang over the prison camp. The fine rain sizzled into steam when it fell on glowing embers.

Kylis started at the long shrill siren that ended the second shift. For an instant she was afraid the hallucinations had returned, but the normal sounds of the prison responded to the signal. The faraway roar of bulldozers ceased; the high whine of the drill slipped down in pitch and finally stopped. People left their machines, threw down their tools, and straggled toward the trail. They passed beneath the guards' towers, watched and counted by the Lizard's crew. One by one and in occasional pairs they started up the steep slope of clay and debris and volcanic ash, picking their way around gullies and across muddy rivulets. Screwtop seemed very quiet now, almost peaceful, with no noise but the hum of turbines in the two geothermal power plants, and the rhythmic clatter of the pumps that kept the drill pit unflooded.

Kylis could not yet see Jason. She frowned. He and Gryf, who was on the third shift, had both been all right when she got off duty. She was sure of that, for news of accidents traveled instantaneously between working crews. But Kylis had been alone, sleeping much of the time, in the nine hours since the end of her shift. Anything could happen in nine hours. She tried to reassure herself about her friends' safety, because the pattern and rhythm of the work just ended had been too normal to follow a really bad accident.

She could not put aside her anxiety and knew she would not until she had seen and spoken to and touched both Gryf and Jason. She still found herself surprised that she could care so much about two other human beings. Her past life had depended on complete independence and self-sufficiency.

Below, Gryf would be standing in the group of prisoners near the drilling rig. She tried to make him out, but the only person she could distinguish at this distance was the guard captain, called by everyone—when he was out of earshot—the Lizard, for his clean-shaven face and head gave him a smoothly impervious reptilian appearance. He was standing alone, facing the prisoners, giving orders. He wore black, as if in defiance of the heat, as a symbol of his superiority over everyone else in the camp. Even so, he was conspicuous now only because he was separated from the others. Gryf was conspicuous in any crowd, but the rig was too far away for Kylis to identify even Gryf's astonishing ebony-and-tan calico-patterned skin. The first time she had seen him, his first day at Screwtop, she had stared at him so long that he noticed and laughed at her. It was not a ridiculing laugh, but an understanding one. Gryf laughed at himself, too, sometimes, and often at the people who had made him what he was.

Gryf was the first tetraparental Kylis had ever seen or heard of, and even among tetras Gryf was unusual. Of his four biological parents, it happened that two of them were dark, and two fair. Gryf had been planned to be a uniform light brown, only his hair, perhaps, varicolored. Genes for hair color did not blend like those for skin. But the sets of sperm and ova had been matched wrong, so the mixture of two embryos forming Gryf made him his strange paisley pattern. He still had all the selectable intellectual gifts of his various parents. Those qualities, not his skin, were important.

New tetraparentals were special; the life of each was fully planned. Gryf was part of a team, and it was inconceivable to the government of Redsun and to the other tetras that after all the work of making him, after all the training and preparation, he would refuse his duty. When he did, he was sent for punishment to Redsun's strictest prison. If he changed his mind, he could at a word return to the tetra's secluded retreat. He had been at Screwtop half a year and he had not said that word.

Kylis was no Redsun native; she was oblivious to the others' awe of Gryf. She was curious about him. Neither because of nor in spite of the pattern of his skin, he was beautiful. Kylis wondered how his hair would feel, the locks half black and wiry, half blond and fine.

He was assigned to a nearby crew. Kylis saw immediately that he had been given hard and dirty jobs, not the most dangerous ones but those most tiring. The guards' task was not to kill him but to make life so unpleasant that he would return to the tetras.

Kylis waited to speak to him until she would not risk discipline for either of them. Without seeming to, the Lizard was watching Gryf closely, padding by every so often in his stealthy, silent way, his close-set eyes heavy-lidded, the direction of his gaze impossible to determine. But eventually his duties took him to another part of the camp, and Kylis left her own work to tell Gryf the tricks experience had taught her to make the labor a little easier.

Their first night together was Gryf's first night at Screwtop. When the shift ended, it seemed natural to walk back to the prisoners' shelters together. They were too tired to do much more than sleep, but the companionship was a comfort and the potential for more existed. They lay facing each other in the darkness. Starlight shone through a break in the clouds and glinted from the blond locks of Gryf's hair.

"I may never be let out of here," Gryf said. He was not asking for sympathy, but telling her his future as best he knew it. He had a pleasant, musical voice. Kylis realized these were the first words she heard him say. But she remembered his thanking her for her advice—and recalled that he had thanked her with his smile and a nod and the look in his eyes.

"I'm in for a long time," Kylis said. "I don't think there's that much difference between us." Screwtop could kill either of them the next day or the day before release.

Kylis reached up and touched Gryf's hair. It was stiff and matted with sweat. He took her hand and kissed her grimy palm. From then on they stayed together, growing closer but never speaking of a future outside the prison.

Several sets later Jason arrived and changed everything.

Kylis brought herself back to the present. She knew Gryf was below somewhere, though she could not make him out in the blotch of dirty white. She had been on the last shift during a previous set and she knew the schedule. The prisoners still working would not be exposed to much more danger today. Instead, they would have the dullest and most exhausting job of the period. During the last shift before the free day, once every forty days, all the equipment was cleaned and inspected. Anything done wrong was done over; the shift could drag on long past its normal end. Kylis hoped that would not happen this time.

At the bottom of the slope, Jason emerged from the bright cancer of machinery. He was muddy and grease-spattered, gold-flecked with bleached hair. He was very large and very fair, and even on Redsun where the light had little ultraviolet he sunburned easily. Though he had been working from dusk to mid-morning his legs were horizontally striped with sunburn, darkest at the top of his thighs and lightest just below his knees, marking the different levels to which he had pulled the cuffs of his boots. Right now they were folded all the way down.

He glanced up and saw Kylis. His carriage changed; he straightened and waved. His blond beard was bristly and uncombed and his hair was plastered down with sweat. The waistband of his shorts was red with mud spattered onto his body and washed down by perspiration and rain. As he came closer she saw that he was thinner, and that the lines around his eyes had deepened. They had been lines of thought and laughter; now they were of fatigue and exposure. He hurried toward her, slipping on the clay, and she realized he, too, had been worried.

He heard I was in sensory deprivation, she thought, and he was afraid for me. She stood motionless for a few seconds. She was not quite used to him yet; his easy acceptance of her and his concern seemed innocent and admirable compared to the persistent distrust Kylis had felt toward him for so long. She started forward to meet him.

He stopped and held out his hands. She touched him, and he came forward, almost trembling, holding himself taut against exhaustion. His pose collapsed. Bending down, he rested his forehead on her shoulder. She put her hands on his back, very gently.

"Was it bad?" His voice was naturally low but now it was rough and hoarse. He had probably been directing his crew, shouting above the roar of machinery for eighteen hours.

"Bad enough," Kylis said. "I've been glad of the work since."

Still leaning against her, he shook his head.

"I'm okay now. I've quit hallucinating," she said, hoping it was true. "And you? Are you all right?" She could feel his breath on her damp shoulder.

"Yes. Now. Thanks to Gryf."

Jason had started this set on first day shift, which began at midnight and ended in the afternoon. Its members worked through the hottest part of the day when they were most tired. Halfway through his third work period Jason had collapsed. He was delirious and dehydrated, sunburned even through his shirt. The sun drained him. Gryf, just getting off when Jason fell, had worked through his own sleep period to finish Jason's shift. For them to switch shifts, Gryf had worked almost two of Redsun's days straight. When Kylis heard about that, she could not see how anyone could do it, even Gryf.

Gryf had broken the rules, but no one had made Jason go back to his original shift. The Lizard must never have said anything about it. Kylis could imagine him standing in shadow, watching, while Gryf waited for a confrontation that never came. It was something the Lizard would do.

Jason's shoulders were scarred where blisters had formed in the sun, but Kylis saw that they had healed cleanly. She put her arm around Jason's waist to support him. "Come on. I found a place to sleep." They were both sticky with sweat and the heat.

"Okay." They crossed the barren mud where all the vegetation had been stripped away so the machines could pass. Before they turned off the path they drew rations from the mechanical dispenser near the prisoners' quarters. The tasteless bars dropped through a slot, two each. There were times in Kylis' life when she had not eaten well, but she had seldom eaten anything as boring as prison rations. Jason put one of his bars into his belt pouch.

"When are you going to give that up?"

Jason nibbled a corner of his second ration bar. "I'm not." His grin made the statement almost a joke. He saved part of his food against what Kylis thought ludicrous plans of escape. When he had saved enough supplies, he was going to hike out through the marsh.

"You don't have to save anything today." She slipped her tag back into the slot and kept reinserting it until the extra points were used and a small pile of ration bars lay in the hopper.

"They forgot to void my card for the time I was in the deprivation box," Kylis said. In sensory deprivation, one of the prison's punishments for mistakes, she had been fed in-

travenously. She gave Jason the extra food.
He thanked her and put it in his belt pouch.
Together they crossed the bare clay and en-
tered the forest.

Jason had been at Screwtop only three
sets. He was losing weight quickly here, for
he was a big-boned man with little fat to
burn. Kylis hoped his family would discover
where he was and ransom him soon. And she
hoped they would find him before he tried to
run away, though she had stopped trying to
argue him out of the dream. The marsh was
impassable except by hovercraft. There were
no solid paths through it, and people claimed
it held undiscovered animals that would
crush a boat or raft. Kylis neither believed
nor disbelieved in the animals; she was certain only that a few prisoners had tried to
escape during her time at Screwtop, and the
guards had not even bothered to look for
them. Redsun was not a place where the authorities allowed escape toward freedom,
only toward death. The naked volcanoes cut
off escape to the north and east with their
barren lava escarpments and billowing
clouds of poison gas; the marsh barred west
and south. Screwtop was an economical
prison, requiring fences only to protect the
guards' quarters and the power domes, not
to enclose the captives. And even if Jason
could escape alive, he could never get off
Redsun. He did not have Kylis' experience at
traveling undetected.

The fern forest's shadows closed in around
them, and they walked between the towering
blackish-red stalks and lacy fronds. The fo-

liage was heavy with huge droplets formed slowly by the misty rain. Kylis brushed past a leaf and the water cascaded down her side, making a faint track in the ashes and mud on her skin. She had washed herself when she got off duty, but staying clean was impossible at Screwtop.

They reached the sleeping place she had discovered. Several clumps of ferns had grown together and died, the stems falling over to make a conical shelter. Kylis pulled aside a handful of withered fronds and showed Jason in. Outside it looked like nothing but a pile of dead plants.

"It isn't even damp," he said, surprised. "And it's almost cool in here." He sat down on the carpet of dead moss and ferns and leaned back smiling. "I don't see how you found it. I never would have looked in here."

Kylis sat beside him. A few hours ago she had slept the soundest sleep she had had in Screwtop. The shade alleviated the heat, and the fronds kept the misty rain from drifting inside and collecting. Best of all, it was quiet.

"I thought you and Gryf would like it."

"Have you seen him?"

"Only across the compound. He looked all right."

Jason said aloud what Kylis feared. "The Lizard must have had a reason for letting him take my shift. To make it harder on him." He too was worried, and Kylis could see he felt guilty. "I shouldn't have let him do it," he said.

"Have you ever tried to stop him from doing something he thinks he should?"

Jason smiled. "No. I don't think I want to." He let himself sink further down in the moss. "Gods," he said, drawing out the word. "It's good to see you."

"It's been lonely," Kylis said, with the quiet sort of wonder she felt every time she realized that she did care enough to miss someone. Loneliness was more painful now, but she was not lonely all the time. She did not know how to feel about her newly discovered pleasure in the company of Gryf and Jason. Sometimes it frightened her. They had broached her defenses of solitude and suspicion, and at times she felt exposed and vulnerable. She trusted them, but there were even more betrayers at Screwtop than there were outside.

"I didn't give you those extra rations so you could save them all," she said. "I gave them to you so you'd stop starving yourself for one day at least."

"We could all get out of here," he said, "if we saved just a little more food." Even at midmorning, beneath the ferns, it was almost too dark to make out his features, but Kylis knew he was not joking. She said nothing. Jason thought the prisoners who fled into the marsh were still alive there; he thought he could join them and be helped. Kylis thought they were all dead. Jason believed escape on foot possible, and Kylis believed it death. Jason was an optimist, and Kylis was experienced.

"All right," Jason said. "I'll eat one more. In a while." He lay down flat and put his hands behind his head.

"How was your shift?" Kylis asked.

"Too much fresh meat."

Kylis grinned. Jason was talking like a veteran, hardened and disdainful of new prisoners, the fresh meat, who had not yet learned the ways of Screwtop.

"We only got a couple new people," she said. "You must have had almost the whole bunch."

"It would have been tolerable if three of them hadn't been assigned to the drilling rig."

"Did you lose any?"

"No. By some miracle."

"We were fresh once too. Gryf's the only one I ever saw who didn't start out doing really stupid things."

"Was I really that fresh?"

She did not want to hurt his feelings or even tease him.

"I was, wasn't I?"

"Jason ... I'm sorry, but you were the freshest I ever saw. I didn't think you had any chance at all. Only Gryf did."

"I hardly remember anything about the first set, except how much time he spent helping me."

"I know," Kylis said. Jason had needed a great deal of help. Kylis had forgiven him for being the cause of her first real taste of loneliness, but she could not quite forget it.

"Gods—this last set," Jason said. "I didn't know how bad it was alone." Then he smiled. "I used to think I was a solitary person." Where Kylis was contemptuous of her discovered weaknesses, Jason was amused at and interested in his. "What did you do before Gryf came?"

"Before Gryf came, I didn't know how bad it was alone, either," she said rather roughly. "You'd better get some sleep."

He smiled. "You're right. Good morning." He fell asleep instantly.

Relaxed, he looked tireder. His hair had grown long enough to tie back, but it had escaped from its knot and curled in tangled, dirty tendrils around his face. Jason hated being dirty, but working with the drill left little energy for extras, like bathing. He would never really adjust to Screwtop as Gryf and Kylis had. His first day here, Gryf had kept him from being killed or crippled at least twice. Kylis had been working on the same shift but a different crew, driving one of the bulldozers and clearing another section of forest. The drill could not be set up among the giant ferns, because the ground itself would not stand much stress. Beneath a layer of humus was clay, so wet that in response to pressure it turned semiliquid, almost like quicksand. The crews had to strip off the vegetation and the layers of clay and volcanic ash until bedrock lay exposed. Kylis drove the dozer back and forth, cutting through ferns in a much wider path than the power plants themselves would have required. She had to make room for the excavated earth, which was piled well back from the Pit's edges. Even so the slopes sometimes collapsed in mudslides.

At the end of the day of Jason's arrival, the siren went off, and Kylis drove the dozer to the old end of the Pit and into the recharging stall. Gryf was waiting for her, and a big fair man was with him, sitting slumped on the ground with his head between his knees and his hands limp on the ground. Kylis hardly noticed him. She took Gryf's hand, to walk with him back to the shelters, but he quietly stopped her and helped the other man to his feet. The new prisoner's expression was blank with exhaustion; in the dawn light he looked deathly pale. Hardly anyone on Redsun was as fair as he, even in the north. Kylis supposed he was from off-world, but he did not have the shoulder tattoo that would have made her trust him instantly. But Gryf was half carrying the big clumsy man, so she supported him on the other side. Together she and Gryf got him to their shelter. He neither ate nor drank nor even spoke, but collapsed on the hard lumpy platform and fell asleep. Gryf watched him with a troubled expression.

"Who is that?" Kylis did not bother to hide the note of contempt in her voice.

Gryf told her the man's name, which was long and complicated and contained a lot of double vowels. She never remembered it all, even now. "He says to call him Jason."

"Did you know him before?" She was willing to help Gryf save an old friend, though she did not quite see how they would do it. In one day he had spent himself completely.

"No," Gryf said. "But I read his work. I never thought I'd get to meet him."

The undisguised awe in Gryf's voice hurt Kylis, not so much because she was jealous as because it reminded her how limited her own skills were. The admiration in the faces of drunks and children in spaceport bazaars, which Kylis had experienced, was nothing compared to Gryf's feeling for the accomplishments of this man.

"Is he in here for writing a book?"

"No, thank gods—they don't know who he is. They think he's a transient. He travels under his personal name instead of his family name. They are making him work for his passage home."

"How long?"

"Six sets."

"Oh, Gryf."

"He must live and be released."

"If he's important, why hasn't anybody ransomed him?"

"His family doesn't know where he is. They would have to be contacted in secret. If the government finds out who he is, they will never let him go. His books are smuggled in."

Kylis shook her head.

"He affected my life, Kylis. He helped me understand the idea of freedom. And personal responsibility. The things you have known all your life from your own experience."

"You mean you wouldn't be here except for him."

"I never thought of it that way, but you are right."

"Look at him, Gryf. This place will grind him up."

Gryf stared somberly at Jason, who slept

so heavily he hardly seemed to breathe. "He should not be here. He's a person who should not be hurt."

"We should?"

"He's different."

Kylis did not say Jason would be hurt at Screwtop. Gryf knew that well enough.

Jason had been hurt, and he had changed. What Gryf had responded to in his work was a pure idealism and innocence that could not exist in captivity. Kylis had been afraid Jason would fight the prison by arming himself with its qualities; she was afraid of what that would do to Gryf. But Jason had survived by growing more mature, by retaining his humor, not by becoming brutal. Kylis had never read a word he had written, but the longer she knew him, the more she liked and admired him.

Now she left him sleeping among the ferns. She had slept as much as she wanted to for the moment. She knew from experience that she had to time her sleeping carefully on the day off. In the timeless environment of space, where she had spent most of her life, Kylis' natural circadian rhythm was about twenty-three hours. A standard day of twenty-four did not bother her, but Redsun's twenty-seven hour rotation made her uncomfortable. She could not afford to sleep too much or too little and return to work exhausted and inattentive. At Screwtop inattention was worth punishment at best, and at worst, death.

She was no longer tired, but she was hungry for anything besides the tasteless prison rations. The vegetation on Redsun, afflicted with a low mutation rate, had not evolved very far. The plants were not yet complex enough to produce fruiting bodies. Some of the stalks and roots, though, were edible.

On Redsun, there were no flowers.

Kylis headed deeper into the shadows of the rain forest. Away from the clearings people had made, the primitive plants reached great heights. Kylis wandered among them, her feet sinking into the soft moist humus. Her footprints remained distinct. She turned and looked back. Only a few paces behind her, seeping water had already formed small pools in the deeper marks of her bootheels.

She wished she and Gryf and Jason had been on the same shift. As it was, half of their precious free time would be spent sleeping and readjusting their time schedules. When Gryf finally got off, they would have less than one day together, even before he rested. Sometimes Kylis felt that the single free day in every forty was more a punishment than if the prisoners had been forced to work their sentences straight through. The brief respite allowed them to remember just how much they hated Screwtop, and just how impossible it was to escape.

Since she could not be with both her friends, she preferred complete solitude. For Kylis it was almost instinctive to make certain no one could follow her. Unfolding the cuffs of her boots, she protected her legs to halfway up her thighs. She did not seal the boots to her shorts because of the heat.

The floor of the forest dipped and rose

gently, forming wide hollows where the rain
collected. Kylis stepped into one of the huge
shallow pools and waded across it, walking
slowly, feeling ahead with her toe before she
put her foot down firmly. The mist and shadows, the reddish sunlight, and the glassy surface created illusions that concealed
occasional deep pits. Where the water lay
still and calm, parasites crawled out of the
earth and swarmed. They normally repro-
duced inside small fishes and primitive am-
phibians, but they were not particular about
their host. They would invade a human body
through a cut or abrasion, causing agonizing
muscle lesions. Sometimes they traveled
slowly to the brain. The forest was no place
to fall into a water hole.

Avoiding one deep spot, Kylis reached the
far bank and stepped out onto a slick out-
cropping of rock where her footprints would
not show. When the stone ended and she re-
entered the frond forest, the ground was
higher and less sodden, although the misty
rain still fell continuously.

The ferns thinned, the ground rose steeply,
and Kylis began to climb. At the top of the
hill the air stirred, and the vegetation was
not so thick. Kylis found some edible shoots,
picked them, and peeled them carefully. The
pulp was spicy and crunchy. The juice, pun-
gent and sour, trickled down her throat. She
picked a few more stalks and tied the small
bundle to her belt. Those that were sporing,
she was careful not to disturb. Edible plants
no longer grew near camp; in fact, nothing

edible grew close enough to Screwtop to reach on any but the free day.

Redsun traveled upright in its circular orbit; it had no seasons. The plants had no sun-determined clock by which to synchronize their reproduction, so a few branches of any one plant or a few plants of any one species would spore while the rest remained asexual. A few days later a different random set would begin. It was not a very efficient method of spreading traits through the gene pool, but it had sufficed until people came along and destroyed fertile plants as well as spored-out ones. Kylis, who had noticed in her wanderings that evolution ceased at the point when human beings arrived and began to make their changes, tried not to cause that kind of damage.

A flash of white, a movement, caught the edge of her vision. She froze, wishing the hallucinations away but certain they had come back. White was not a natural color in the frond forest, not even the muddy pink that passed for white under Redsun's enormous star. But no strange fantasy creatures paraded around her; she heard no furious imaginary sounds. Her feet remained firmly on the ground, the warm fine rain hung around her, the ferns drooped with their burden of droplets. Slowly Kylis turned until she faced the direction of the motion. She was not alone.

She moved quietly forward until she could look through the black foliage. What she had seen was the uniform of Screwtop, white boots, white shorts, white shirt for anyone with a reason to wear it. One of the other prisoners sat on a rock, looking out across the forest, toward the swamp. Tears rolled slowly down her face, though she made no sound. Miria.

Feeling only a little guilty about invading her privacy, Kylis watched her, as she had been watching her for some time. Kylis thought Miria was a survivor, someone who would leave Screwtop without being broken. She kept to herself; she had no partners. Kylis had admired her tremendous capacity for work. She was taller than Kylis, bigger, potentially stronger, but clearly unaccustomed to great physical labor. For a while she had worn her shirt tied up under her breasts, but like most others she had discarded it because of the heat.

Miria survived in the camp without using other people or allowing herself to be used. Except when given a direct order, she acted as if the guards simply did not exist, in effect defying them without giving them a reasonable excuse to punish her. They did not always wait for reasonable excuses. Miria received somewhat more than her share of pain, but her dignity remained intact.

Kylis retreated a couple of steps, then came noisily out of the forest, giving Miria a few seconds to wipe away her tears if she wanted to. But when Kylis stopped, pretending to be surprised at finding another person so near, Miria simply turned toward her.

"Hello, Kylis."

Kylis went closer. "Is anything wrong?"

That was such a silly question that she added, "I mean, is there anything I can do?"

Miria's smile erased the lines of tension in her forehead and revealed laugh lines Kylis had never noticed before. "No," Miria said. "Nothing anyone can do. But thank you."

"I guess I'd better go."

"Please don't," Miria said quickly. "I'm so tired of being alone—" She cut herself off and turned away, as if she were sorry to have revealed so much of herself. Kylis knew how she felt. She sat down nearby.

Miria looked out again over the forest. The fronds were a soft reddish black. The marsh trees were harsher, darker, interspersed with gray patches of water. Beyond the marsh, over the horizon, lay an ocean that covered all of Redsun except the large inhabited North Continent and the tiny South Continent where the prison camp lay.

Kylis could see the ugly scar of the pits where the crews were still drilling, but Miria had her back half turned and she gazed only at unspoiled forest.

"It could all be so beautiful," Miria said.

"Do you really think so?" Kylis thought it ugly—the black foliage, the dim light, the day too long, the heat, no animals except insects that did not swim or crawl. Redsun was the most nearly intolerable planet she had ever been on.

"Yes. Don't you?"

"No. I don't see any way I ever could."

"It's sometimes hard, I know," Miria said. "Sometimes, when I'm tiredest, I even feel the same. But the world's so rich and so strange—don't you see the challenge?''

"I only want to leave it," Kylis said.

Miria looked at her for a moment, then nodded. "You're not from Redsun, are you?"

Kylis shook her head.

"No, there's no reason for you to have the same feelings as someone born here."

This was a side of Miria that Kylis had never seen, one of quiet but intense dedication to a world whose rulers had imprisoned her. Despite her liking for Miria, Kylis was confused. "How can you feel that way when they've sent you here? I hate them, I hate this place—"

"Were you wrongly arrested?" Miria asked with sympathy.

"They could have just deported me. That's what usually happens."

"Sometimes injustice is done," Miria said sadly. "I know that. I wish it wouldn't happen. But I deserve to be here, and I know that too. When my sentence is completed, I'll be forgiven."

More than once Kylis had thought of staying on some world and trying to live the way other people did, even of accepting punishment, if necessary, but what had always stopped her was the doubt that forgiveness was often, or ever, fully given. Redsun seemed an unlikely place to find amnesty.

"What did you do?"

Kylis felt Miria tense and wished she had not asked. Not asking questions about the past was one of the few tacit rules among the prisoners.

"I'm sorry . . . it's not that I wouldn't tell you, but I just cannot talk about it."

Kylis sat in silence for a few minutes, scuffing the toe of her boot along the rock like an anxious child and rubbing the silver tattoo on the point of her left shoulder. The pigment caused irritation and slight scarring. The intricate design had not hurt for a long time, nor even itched, but she could feel the delicate lines. Rubbing them was a habit. Even though the tattoo represented a life to which she would probably never return, it was soothing.

"What's that?" Miria asked. Abruptly she grimaced. "I'm sorry, I'm doing just what I asked you not to do."

"It doesn't matter," Kylis said. "I don't mind. It's a spaceport rat tattoo. You get it when the other rats accept you." Despite everything, she was proud of the mark.

"What's a spaceport rat?"

That Miria was unfamiliar with the rats did not surprise Kylis. Few Redsun people had heard of them. On almost every other world Kylis ever visited, the rats were, if not exactly esteemed, at least admired. Some places she had been actively worshiped. Even where she was officially unwelcome, the popular regard was high enough to prevent the kind of entrapment Redsun had started.

"I used to be one. It's what everybody calls people who sneak on board starships and live in them and in spaceports. We travel all over."

"That sounds . . . interesting," Miria said. "But didn't it bother you to steal like that?"

A year before, Kylis would have laughed at the question, even knowing, as she did, that Miria was quite sincere. But recently Kylis had begun to wonder: Might something be more important than outwitting space-port security guards? While she was wondering, she came to Redsun, so she never had a chance to find out.

"I started when I was ten," Kylis said to Miria. "So I didn't think of it like that."

"You sneaked onto a starship when you were only ten?"

"Yes."

"All by yourself?"

"Until the others start to recognize you, no one will help you much. It's possible. And I thought it was my only chance to get away from where I was."

"You must have been in a terrible place."

"It's hard to remember if it was really as bad as I think. I can remember my parents, but never smiling, only yelling at each other and hitting me."

Miria shook her head. "That's terrible, to be driven away by your own people—to have nowhere to grow up. . . . Did you ever go back?"

"I don't think so."

"What?"

"I can't remember much about where I was born. I always thought I'd recognize the spaceport, but there might have been more than one, so maybe I have been back and maybe I haven't. The thing is, I can't remember what they called the planet. Maybe I never knew."

"I cannot imagine it—not to know who you are or where you come from or even who your parents were."

"I know *that*," Kylis said.

"You could find out about the world. Fingerprints or ship records or regression—"

"I guess I could. If I ever wanted to. Sometime I might even do it, if I ever get out of here."

"I'm sorry we stopped you. Really. It's just that we feel that everyone who can should contribute a fair share."

Kylis still found it hard to believe that after being sent to Screwtop Miria would include herself in Redsun's collective conscience, but she had said "we." Kylis only thought of authorities as "they."

She shrugged. "Spaceport rats know they can get caught. It doesn't happen too often and usually you hear that you should avoid the place."

"I wish you had."

"We take the chance." She touched the silver tattoo again. "You don't get one of these until you've proved you can be trusted. So when places use informers against us, we usually know who they are."

"But on Redsun you were betrayed?"

"I never expected them to use a child," Kylis said bitterly.

"A child!"

"This little kid sneaked on my ship. He did a decent job of it, and he reminded me of me. He was only ten or eleven, and he was all beat up. I guess we aren't so suspicious of kids because most of us started at the same age." Kylis glanced at Miria and saw that she was staring at her, horrified.

"They used a child? And injured him, just to catch you?"

"Does that really surprise you?"

"Yes," Miria said.

"Miria, half the people who were killed during the last set weren't more than five or six years older than the boy who turned me in. Most of the people being sent here now are that age. What could they possibly have done terrible enough to get them sent here?"

"I don't know," Miria said softly without looking up. "We need the power generators. Someone has to drill the steam wells. Some of us will die in the work. But you're right about the young people. I've been thinking about . . . other things. I had not noticed." She said that as if she had committed a crime, or more exactly a sin, by not noticing. "And the child . . ." Her voice trailed off and she smiled sadly at Kylis. "How old are you?"

"I don't know. Maybe twenty."

Miria raised one eyebrow. "Twenty? Older in experience, but not that old in time. You should not be here."

"But I am. I'll survive it."

"I think you will. And what then?"

"Gryf and Jason and I have plans."

"On Redsun?"

"Gods, no."

"Kylis," Miria said carefully, "you do not know much about tetraparentals, do you?"

"How much do I need to know?"

"I was born here. I used to . . . to work for

them. Their whole purpose is their intelligence. Normal people like you and me bore them. They cannot tolerate us for long."

"Miria, stop it!"

"Your friend will only cause you pain. Give him up. Put him away from you. Urge him to go home."

"No! He knows I'm an ordinary person. We know what we're going to do."

"It makes no difference," Miria said with abrupt coldness. "He will not be allowed to leave Redsun."

Kylis felt the blood drain from her face. No one had ever said that so directly and brutally before. "They can't keep him. How long will they make him stay here before they realize they can't break him?"

"He is important. He owes Redsun his existence."

"But he's a person with his own dreams. They can't make him a slave!"

"His research team is worthless without him."

"I don't care," Kylis said.

"*You*—" Miria cut herself off. Her voice became much gentler. "They will try to persuade him to follow their plans. He may decide to do as they ask."

"I wouldn't feel any obligation to the people who run things on Redsun even if I lived here. Why should he be loyal to them? Why should you? What did they ever do but send you here? What will they let you do when you get out? Anything decent or just more dirty, murderous jobs like this one?" She realized she was shouting, and Miria looked stunned.

"I don't know," Miria said. "I don't know, Kylis. Please stop saying such dangerous things." She was terrified and shaken, much more upset than when she had been crying.

Kylis moved nearer and took her hand. "I'm sorry, Miria, I didn't mean to hurt you or say anything that could get you in trouble." She paused, wondering how far Miria's fear of Redsun's government might take her from her loyalty.

"Miria," she said on impulse, "have you ever thought of partnering with anybody?"

Miria hesitated so long that Kylis thought she would not answer. Kylis wondered if she had intruded on Miria's past again.

"No," Miria finally said. "Never."

"Would you?"

"Think about it? Or do it?"

"Both. Partner with me and Gryf and Jason. Not just here, but when we get out."

"No," Miria said. "No, I couldn't." She sounded frightened again.

"Because we want to leave Redsun?"

"Other reasons."

"Would you just think about it?"

Miria shook her head.

"I know you don't usually live in groups on Redsun," Kylis said. "But where I was born, a lot of people did, even though my parents were alone. I remember, before I ran away, my friends were never afraid to go home like I was. Jason spent all his life in a group family, and he says it's a lot easier to get along." She was skipping over her own

occasional doubts that any world could be as
pleasant as the one Jason described. Whatever it was like, it had to be better than her
own former existence of constant hiding and
constant uncertainty; it had to be better than
what Gryf told her of Redsun, with its em-
phasis on loyalty to the government at the
expense of any family structure too big to
move instantly at the whim or order of the
rulers.

Miria did not respond.

"Anyway, three people aren't enough—we
thought we'd find others after we got out.
But I think—"

"Gryf doesn't—" Miria interrupted Kylis,
then stopped herself and started over. "They
don't know you were going to ask me?"

"Not exactly, but they both know you,"
Kylis said defensively. She thought Miria
might be afraid Kylis' partners would refuse
her. Kylis knew they would not but could not
put how she knew into proper words.

The rain had blurred away the marks of
tears on Miria's cheeks, and now she smiled
and squeezed Kylis' hand. "Thank you,
Kylis," she said. "I wish I could accept. I
can't, but not for the reasons you think.
You'll find someone better." She started up,
but Kylis stopped her.

"No, you stay here. This is your place."
Kylis stood. "If you change your mind, just
say. All right?"

"I won't change my mind."

"I wish you wouldn't be so sure." Reluctantly, she started away.

"Kylis?"

"Yes?"

"Please don't tell anyone you asked me this."

"Not even Gryf and Jason?"

"No one. Please."

"All right," Kylis said unwillingly.

Kylis left Miria on the stony hillside. She glanced back once before entering the forest. Miria was sitting on the stone again, hunched forward, her forearms on her knees. Now she was looking down at the huge slash of clay and trash heaps, the complicated delicate cooling towers that condensed the generators' steam, the high impervious antenna beaming power north toward the cities.

When Kylis reached the sleeping place, the sun was high. Beneath the dead fern trees it was still almost cool. She crept in quietly and sat down near Jason without waking him. He lay sprawled in dry moss, breathing deeply, solid and real. As if he could feel her watching him, he half opened his eyes.

Kylis lay down and drew her hand up his side, feeling bones that had become more prominent, dry and flaking sunburned skin, and the scabs of cuts and scratches. He was bruised as though the guards had beaten him, perhaps because of his occasional amusement at things so odd that his reaction seemed insolence. But for now, she would not notice his new scars, and he would not notice hers.

"Are you awake?"

He laughed softly. "I think so."

"Do you want to go back to sleep?"

He reached out and touched her face. "I'm not that tired."

Kylis smiled and leaned over to kiss him. The hairs of his short beard were soft and stiff against her lips and tongue. For a while she and Jason could ignore the heat.

Lying beside Jason, not quite touching because the afternoon was growing hot, Kylis only dozed while Jason again slept soundly. She sat up and pulled on her shorts and boots, brushed a lock of Jason's sunstreaked hair from his damp forehead, and slipped outside. A couple of hours of Gryf's work shift remained, so Kylis headed toward the guards' enclosure and the hovercraft dock.

Beyond the drill-pit clearing, the forest extended for a short distance westward. The ground continued to fall, growing wetter and wetter, changing perceptibly into marsh. The enclosure, a hemispherical electrified fence completely covering the guards' residence domes, was built at the juncture of relatively solid land and shallow, standing water. It protected the hovercraft ramp, and it was invulnerable. She had tried to get through it. She had even tried to dig beneath it. Digging under a fence or cutting through one was something no spaceport rat would do, short of desperation. After her first few days at Screwtop, Kylis had been desperate. She had not believed she could survive her sentence in the prison. So, late one night, she crept over to the electrified fence and began to dig. At dawn she had not reached the bottom of the fence supports, and the ground was wet enough to start carrying electricity to her in small warning tingles.

Her shift would begin soon; guards would be coming in and going out, and she would be caught if she did not stop. She planned to cover over the hole she had dug and hope it was not discovered.

She was lying flat on the ground, digging a narrow deep hole with a flat rock and both hands, smeared all over with the red clay, her fingernails ripped past the quick. She reached down for one last handful of dirt, and grabbed a trap wire.

The current swept through her, contracting every muscle in her body. It lasted only an instant. She lay quivering, almost insensible, conscious enough to be glad the wire had been set to stun, not kill. She tried to get up and run, but she could not move properly. She began to shudder again. Her muscles were overstimulated, incapable of distinguishing a real signal. She ached all over, so badly that she could not even guess if the sudden clench of muscles had broken any bones.

A light shone toward her. She heard footsteps as the guards approached to investigate the alarm the trap wire had set off. The sound thundered through her ears, as though the electric current had heightened all her senses, toward pain. The footsteps stopped; the light beam blinded her, then left her face. Her dazzled vision blurred the figure standing over her, but she knew it was the Lizard. It occurred to her, in a vague, slow-motion thought, that she did not know his real name.

(She learned later that no one else did either.) He dragged Kylis to her feet and held her upright, glaring at her, his face taut with anger and his eyes narrow.

"Now you know we're not as easy to cheat as starship owners," he said. His voice was low and raspy, softly hoarse. He let her go, and she collapsed again. "You're on probation. Don't make any more mistakes. And don't be late for duty."

The other guards followed him away. They did not even bother to fill in the hole she had dug.

Kylis had staggered through that workday; she survived it, and the next, and the next, until she knew that the work itself would not kill her. She did not try to dig beneath the fence again, but she still watched the hovercraft when it arrived.

By the time she reached her place of concealment on the bank above the fence, the hovercraft had already climbed the ramp and settled. The gate was locked behind it. Kylis watched the new prisoners being unloaded. The cargo bay door swung open. The people staggered out on deck and down the gangway, disoriented by the long journey in heat and darkness. One of the prisoners stumbled and fell to his knees, retching.

Kylis remembered how she had felt after so many hours in the pitch-dark hold. Even talking was impossible, for the engines were on the other side of the hold's interior bulkhead and the fans were immediately below. She was too keyed up to go into a trance, and a trance would be dangerous while she was crowded in with so many people.

The noise was what Kylis remembered most about coming to Screwtop—incessant, penetrating noise, the high whine of the engines and the roar of the fans. She had been half deaf for days afterward. The compartment was small. Despite the heat the prisoners could not avoid sitting and leaning against each other, and as soon as the engines started, the temperature began to rise. By the time the hovercraft reached the prison, the hold was thick with the stench of human misery. Kylis hardly noticed when the craft's sickening swaying ceased. When the hatch opened and red light spilled in, faintly dissipating the blackness, Kylis looked up with all the others, and, like all the others, blinked like a frightened animal.

The guards had no sympathy for cramped muscles or nausea. Their shouted commands faded like faraway echoes through Kylis' abused hearing. She pushed herself up, using the wall as support. Her legs and feet were asleep. They began regaining sensation, and she felt as if she were walking on tiny knives. She hobbled out, but at the bottom of the gangway she, too, had stumbled. A guard's curse and the prod of his club brought her to her feet in a fury, fists clenched, but she quelled her violent temper instantly. The guard watched with a smile, waiting. But Kylis had been to earth, where one of the few animals left alive outside the game preserves and zoos was the possum. She had learned its lesson well.

Now she crouched on the bank and watched the new prisoners realize, as she had, that the end of the trip did not end the terrible heat. Screwtop was almost on the equator of Redsun, and the heat and humidity never lessened. Even the rain was lukewarm.

The guards prodded the captives into a compact group and turned hoses on them, spraying off filth and sweat. Afterward the new people plodded through the mud to the processing dome. Kylis watched each one pass through the doorway. She had never defined what she looked for when she watched the new arrivals, but whatever it was, she did not find it today. Even more of them were terribly young, and they all had the look of hopelessness that would make them nothing more than fresh meat, new bodies for the work to use up. Screwtop would grind them down and throw them away. They would die of disease or exhaustion or carelessness. Kylis did not see in one of them the spark of defiance that might get them through their sentences intact in body or spirit. But sometimes the spark only came out later, exposed by the real adversity of the work.

The hatch swung shut and the hovercraft's engines roared to full power. No one at all had been taken on board for release on North Continent.

The boat quivered on its skirts and floated back down the ramp, through the entrance, onto the glassy gray surface of the water. The gate sparked shut. Kylis was vaguely disappointed, for the landing was no differ-

ent from any she had seen since she was
brought to Screwtop herself. There was no
way to get on board the boat. The familiar
admission still annoyed her. For a spaceport
rat, admitting defeat to the safeguards of an
earthbound vehicle was humiliating. She
could not even think of a way to get herself
out of Screwtop, much less herself and Gryf
and Jason. She was afraid that if she did not
find some chance of escape, Jason might really try to flee through the swamp.

She ran her fingers through her short
black hair and shook her head, flinging out
the misty rain that gathered in huge drops
and slipped down her face and neck and
back. The heat and the rain—she hated both.

In an hour or two the evening rain would
fall in solid sheets, washing the mist away.
But an hour after that the faint infuriating
droplets would begin again. They seemed
never to fall, but hung in the air and collected on skin, on hair, beneath trees, inside
shelters.

Kylis grabbed an overhanging plant and
stripped off a few of its red-black fronds,
flinging them to the ground in anger.

She stood up, but suddenly crouched down
in hiding again. Below, Miria walked up to
the fence, placed her hand against the palm
lock, and waited, glancing over her shoulder
as if making certain she was alone. As the
gate swung open and Miria, a prisoner,
walked alone and free into the guards' enclosure, Kylis felt her knees grow weak. Miria
stopped at a dome, and the door opened for

her. Kylis thought she could see the Lizard in the dimness beyond.

Almost the only thing this could mean was that Miria was a spy. Kylis began to tremble in fear and anger, fear of what Miria could tell the Lizard that would help him increase the pressure on Gryf, anger at herself for trusting Miria. She had made another mistake in judgment like the one that had imprisoned her, and this time the consequences could be much worse.

She sat in the mud and the rain trying to think, until she realized that Gryf would be off work in only a few minutes. She did not even have time to wake Jason.

When Kylis turned her back on the guards' domes, Miria had not yet come out.

Kylis was a few minutes late reaching the drill pit. The third shift had already ended; all the prisoners were out and drifting away. Gryf was nowhere around, and he was nothing if not conspicuous. She began to worry, because Gryf was frequently first out, never last—he appeared never to tire. Certainly he would wait for her.

She stood indecisively, worried, thinking, He might have wanted something in the shelter.

She did not believe that for a moment. She glanced back toward the bottom of the Pit.

Everything happened at once. She forgot about Miria, Lizard, the prison. She cried out for Jason, knowing her voice would not carry that far. She ran downhill, fighting the clay that sucked at her feet. Two people she knew slightly trudged up the hill—Troi, skeletal, sharp-featured, sardonic, and Chuzo, squarely built and withdrawn. Both were very young; both were aging quickly here.

They supported Gryf between them.

Ash and grease disguised the pattern of his paisley skin. Kylis knew he was alive only because no one at Screwtop would spend any energy on someone who was dead. When she was closer, she could see the ends of deep slashes made by the whip where it had curled around his body. Blood had dried in narrow streaks on his sides. His wrists were abraded where he had been tied for the punishment.

"Oh, Gryf—"

Hearing her, Gryf raised his head. She felt great relief.

Troi and Chuzo stopped when Kylis reached them.

"The Lizard ordered it himself," Troi said bitterly. Screwtop held few amenities, but people were seldom flogged on the last day of the shift.

"Why?"

"I don't know. I was too far away. Anything. Nothing. What reason do they ever have?"

Kylis quieted her anger for the moment. She took over for Chuzo. "Thank you," she said, quite formally.

Troi stayed where he was. "Get him to the top, anyway," he said in his gruff manner.

"Gryf? Can you make it?"

He tightened his hand on her shoulder. They started up the steep path. When they finally reached the top, the immense sun had set. The sky was pink and scarlet in the west, and the volcanoes eastward glowed blood red.

"Thanks," Kylis said again. Chuzo hesitated, but Troi nodded and left. After a moment Chuzo followed him.

Gryf leaned heavily on her, but she could support him. She tried to turn toward the shelters and their meager stock of medical supplies, but he resisted weakly and guided her toward the waterfall. If he wanted to go there first, he must think his wounds had been contaminated.

"Gods," Kylis whispered. Clumsily, they hurried. She wished Jason had heard her, for with him they could have gone faster. It was her fault he was not there. She could not hold Gryf up alone without hurting his back.

Gryf managed a smile, just perceptible, telling her, I hurt but I am strong.

Yes, Kylis thought, stronger than Jason, stronger than me. We'll survive.

They continued.

"Kylis! Gryf!"

Gryf stopped. Kylis let him, with relief. Jason splashed toward them.

Gryf's knees buckled. Kylis strained to keep him out of the mud, away from more parasites. Jason reached them and picked Gryf up.

"Could you hear me?" Kylis asked.

"No," Jason said. "I woke up and came looking. Where are you taking him?"

"To the overflow pipe."

Jason needed no explanation of the dangers of infection. He carried Gryf toward the waterfall, swearing softly.

The cooling towers from the steam wells produced the only safe water the prisoners had for bathing. It spewed from a pipe to a concrete platform and spilled from there to the ground, forming a muddy pool that spread into the forest. The water was too hot for anyone to go directly beneath the cascade. Jason stopped in knee-deep hot water. They were all standing in heavy spray.

Jason held Gryf against his chest while Kylis splashed water on Gryf's back from her cupped hands. She washed him as gently as she could and still be safe. She found no parasites and none of their eggs. The water swept away mud and sweat, turning Jason bright pink and Kylis auburn and Gryf all shades of dark brown and tan.

Kylis cursed the Lizard. He knew he would look bad in the eyes of the tetra committee if Gryf were crushed or bled to death or went home with everything but his brain. But he would look worse if he could not force Gryf to go home at all.

Gryf's eyelids flickered. His eyes were bright blue, flecked irregularly with black.

"How do you feel?"

He smiled, but he had been hurt—she could see the memory of pain. They had touched his spirit. He looked away from her and made Jason let him turn. He staggered. His knees would not support him, which seemed to surprise him. Jason held him up, and Gryf took the last thin flake of antiseptic soap from Kylis' hand.

"What's the matter?" she asked.

Gryf turned her around. For a moment his touch was painful, then she felt the sharp sting of soap on raw flesh. Gryf showed her his hand, which glittered with a mass of tiny, fragile eggs like mica flakes. Gryf used up her soap scrubbing her side, and Jason got out what soap he had left.

"This cut's pretty deep but it's clean now. You must have fallen and smashed a nest."

"I don't remember—" She had a kinesthetic memory, from running down into the Pit. "Yes, I do . . ." It hit her then, a quick shock of the fear of what might have been— paralysis, senility, agony—if Gryf had not noticed, if the eggs had healed beneath her skin and hatched. Kylis shuddered.

They returned to the compound, supporting Gryf between them. The wall-less, stilt-legged shelters were almost deserted.

Jason climbed the slanted ladder to their shelter backward, leaning against it for stability while he helped Gryf. The steps were slick with yellow lichen. Kylis chinned herself onto the platform. In their floor locker she had to paw through little stacks of Jason's crumbling ration bars before she found their mold poultice and the web box. She had been very hungry, but she had never eaten any of her friend's hoarded food. She would not have had such restraint a year ago.

Jason put Gryf down between the makeshift partitions that marked their section of the shelter. Gryf was pale beneath the pattern of tan and pigment. Kylis almost wished Troi and Chuzo had left him in the Pit. The

Lizard might then have been forced to put him in the hospital. She wondered if Troi or Chuzo might be helping the Lizard make Screwtop as hard on Gryf as they could. She did not want to believe that, but she did not want to believe Miria was an informer, either.

Their spider—Kylis thought of it as a spider, though it was a Redsun-evolved creature—skittered up the corner post to a new web. Kylis often imagined the little brown-mottled creature hanging above them on her tiny fringed feet, hating them. Yet she was free to crawl down the stilt and into the jungle, or to spin a glider and float away, and she never did. In dreams, Kylis envied her; awake, she named her Stupid. Kylis hoped the web box held enough silk to soothe Gryf's back.

"Hey," Jason said, "this stuff is ready."

"Okay." Kylis took the bowl of greenish mold paste. "Gryf?"

He glanced up. His eyelashes and eyebrows were black and blond, narrowly striped.

"Hang on, it might hurt."

He nodded.

Jason held Gryf's hands while Kylis applied first the mold, then delicate strips of spider silk. Gryf did not move. Even now he had enough strength to put aside the pain.

When she was done, Jason stroked Gryf's forehead and gave him water. He did not want to eat, even broth, so they kissed him and sat near him, for his reassurance and their own, until he fell asleep. That did not take long. When he was breathing deeply, Jason got up and went to Kylis, carrying the bowl.

"I want to look at that cut."

"Okay," Kylis said, "but don't use all the paste."

The poultice burned coldly, and Jason's hands were cool on her skin. She sat with her forearms on her drawn-up knees, accepting the pain rather than ignoring it. When he had finished treating her, she took the bowl and daubed the mold on his cuts. She almost told Jason about Miria, but finally decided not to. Kylis had created the problem; she wanted to solve it herself if she could. And, she admitted, she was ashamed of her misjudgment. She could think of no explanation for Miria's actions that would absolve her.

Jason yawned widely.

"Give me your tag and go back to sleep," Kylis said. Since she had been the first to get off work this time, it was her turn to collect their rations. She took Gryf's tag from his belt pouch and jumped from the edge of the platform to the ground.

Kylis approached the ration dispenser cautiously. On Redsun, violent criminals were sent to rehabilitation centers, not to work camps. Kylis was glad of that, though she did not much like to remember the stories of obedient, blank-eyed people coming out of rehab.

Still, some prisoners were confident or foolish or desperate enough to try to overpower others and steal. At Screwtop it was safest to collect neither obligations nor

hatreds. Vengeance was much too simple
here. The underground society of spaceport
rats had not been free of psychopaths; Kylis
knew how to defend herself. Here she had
never had to resort to more serious mea-
sures. If she did, the drill pit was a quick
equalizer between a bully and a smaller person. Mistakes could be planned; machines
malfunctioned.

The duty assignments were posted on the
ration dispenser. Kylis read them and was
astonished and overjoyed to find herself and
her friends all on the same shift, the night
shift. She hurried back to tell them the news,
but Jason was sound asleep, and she did not
have the heart to wake him. Gryf had gone.

Kylis threw the rations in the floor locker
and sat on the edge of the platform. A scav-
enger insect crawled across the lumpy floor
of fern stalks. Kylis caught it and let it go
near Stupid, barricading it until the spider,
stalking, left her new web and seized the insect, paralyzed it, wrapped it in silk to store
it, and dragged it away. Kylis wondered if
their spider ever slept, or if spiders even
needed sleep. Then she stole the web.

She grew worried. She knew Gryf could
take care of himself. He always did. He had
probably never really reached his limits, but
Gryf might overestimate even his strength
and endurance. He had rested barely an
hour.

Kylis fidgeted for a little while longer. Finally she slid down into the mud again.

Water seeped quickly into new footprints
in the battered earth around the shelters;

Gryf had left no trail that she could distinguish from the other marks in the clay. She went into the forest, with some knowledge and some intuition of where he might be. Above her, huge insects flitted past, barely brushing clawed wingtips against the ferns. It was dark, and the star path, streaked across the sky like the half-circular support of a globe, gave a dim yellow light through broken clouds.

Kylis was startled and frightened by a tickling of the short hair at the back of her neck. She flinched and turned. Gryf looked down at her, smiling, amused.

"Kylis, my friend, you really needn't worry about me all the time." She was always surprised, when he spoke, to remember how pleasant and calming his voice was.

His eyes were dilated so the iris was only a narrow circle of light and dark striations.

Every few sets, someone died from sucking slime. It grew in the forest, in small patches like purple jellyfish. It was hallucinogenic, and it was poisonous. Kylis had argued with Gryf about his using it, before her sentence in the sensory deprivation chamber showed her what Screwtop was like for Gryf all the time.

"Gryf—"

"Don't reproach me!"

"I won't," Kylis said, "Not anymore."

Her response startled him only for a moment; that it startled him at all revealed how completely drained he really was. He nodded and put his arms around her.

"Now you know," he said, with sympathy

and understanding. "How long did they make you stay in the box?"

"Eight days. That's what they said, anyway."

He passed his hand across her hair, just touching it. "My poor friend. It seems so much longer."

"It doesn't matter. It's over for me." She almost believed the hallucinations had stopped, but she wondered if she would ever be certain they would never return.

"Do you think the Lizard sentenced you because of me?"

"I don't know. I guess he'd use anything he could if he thought it'd work. Never mind. I'm all right."

"I would have done what they want, but I could not. Can you believe I tried?"

"Do you think I wanted you to?" She touched his face, tracing bone structure with her fingers like someone blind. She could feel the difference between the blond and black hair in his striped eyebrows, but the texture of his skin was smooth. She drew her fingers from his temples to the corners of his jaw, to the tendons of his neck and the tension-knotted muscles of his shoulders. "No one should make friends here," she said.

He smiled, closing his eyes, understanding her irony. "We would lose our souls if we did not."

He turned away abruptly and sat down on a large rock with his head between his knees, struggling against nausea. The new scars did not seem to hurt him. He breathed deeply for some time, then sat up slowly.

"How is Jason?"

"Fine. Recovered. You didn't have to take his shift. Lizard couldn't let him die like that."

"I think the Lizard collects methods of death."

Kylis remembered Miria with a quick shock of returning fear. "Oh, gods, Gryf, what's the use of fighting them?"

Gryf drew her closer. "The use is that you and Jason will not let them destroy you and I believe I am stronger than those who wish to keep me here, and justified in wishing to make my own mistakes rather than theirs." He held out his hand, pale-swirled in the darkness. It was long and fine. Kylis reached out and rubbed it, his wrist, his tense forearm. Gryf relaxed slightly, but Kylis was still afraid. She had never felt frightened before, not like this. But Miria, uncertainty, seeing Gryf hurt, had all combined to make her doubt the possibility of a future.

Gryf was caught and shaken by another spasm of retching. This time he could not suppress it, and it was more severe because he had not eaten. Kylis stood by, unable to do anything but hold his shoulders and hope he would survive the drug this time, as he had all the times before. The dry vomiting was replaced by a fit of coughing. Sweat dripped from his face and down his sides. When the pitch of his coughing rose and his breath grew more ragged, Kylis realized he was sobbing. On her knees beside him, she tried to soothe him. She did not know if he was crying from the sickness, from some

vision she would never see, or from despair.
She held him until, gradually, he was able to
stop.

Sparkles of starlight passed between the
clouds, mottling Gryf with a third color. He
lay face down on the smooth stone, hands
flat against it, cheek pressed to the rock.
Kylis knew how he felt, drained, removed,
heavy.

"Kylis . . . I never slept before like this . . ."

"I won't go far."

She hoped he heard her. She sat cross-
legged on the wide rock beside him, watching
slow movements of muscle as he breathed.
His roan eyelashes were very long and
touched with sweat droplets. The deep welts
in his back would leave scars. Kylis' back
had similar scars, but she felt that the marks
she carried were a brand of shame, while
Gryf's meant defiance and pride. She reached
toward him, but drew back when her hand's
vague shadow touched his face.

When she was certain he was sleeping easily, she left him and went to look nearby for
patches of the green antibiotic mold. Their
supply was exhausted. It was real medicine,
not a superstition. Its active factor was syn-
thesized back north and exported.

Being allowed to walk away from Screwtop, however briefly, made remaining almost
endurable, but the privilege had a more important purpose. It was a constant reminder
of freedom. The short moment of respite only
strengthened the need to get out, and, more
important, the need never to come back.
Redsun knew how to reinforce obedience.

Kylis wandered, never going very far from Gryf, looking for green mold and finding the rarer purple hallucinogenic slime instead. She tried to deny that it tempted her. She could have taken some to Gryf—she almost did—but in the end she left it under the rocks where it belonged.

"I want to talk to you."

She spun, startled, recognizing the rough voice, fearing it, concealing her fear badly. She did not answer, only looked toward the Lizard.

"Come sit with me," he said. Starlight glinted on his clean fingernails as he gestured to the other end of an immense uprooted fern tree. It sagged but held when he sat on it.

As always, his black protective boots were pulled up and sealed to his black shorts. He was even bigger than Jason, taller, heavier, and though he had allowed his body to go slightly to fat, his face had remained narrow and hard. His clean-shaven scalp and face never tanned or burned, but somehow remained pale, in contrast to his deep-set black eyes. He licked his thin lips quickly with the tip of his tongue.

"What do you want?" She did not approach him.

He leaned forward and leaned his forearms on his knees. "I've been watching you."

She had no answer. He watched everyone. Standing there before him, Kylis was uneasy for reasons that somehow had nothing to do with his capacity for brutality. The Lizard never acted this way. He was direct and abrupt.

"I made a decision when sensory deprivation didn't break you," he said. "That was the last test."

The breeze shifted slightly. Kylis smelled a sharp odor as the Lizard lifted a small pipe to his lips and drew on it deeply. He held his breath and offered the pipe to her.

She wanted some. It was good stuff. She and Gryf and Jason had used the last of theirs at the end of the previous set, the night before they went on different shifts. Kylis was surprised that the Lizard used it at all. She would never have expected him to pare off the corners of his aggression out here. She shook her head.

"No?" He shrugged and put the pipe down, letting it waste, burning unattended. "All right."

She let the silence stretch on, hoping he would forget her and whatever he wanted to say, wander off or get hungry or go to sleep.

"You've got a long time left to stay here," he said.

Again, Kylis had no answer.

"I could make it easier for you."

"You could make it easier for most of us."

"That's not my job." He ignored the contradiction.

"What are you trying to say?"

"I've been looking for someone like you for a long time. You're strong, and you're stubborn." He got up and came toward her, hesitated to glance back at his pipe but left it where it was. He took a deep breath. He was trying so hard to look sincere that Kylis had an almost overwhelming urge to laugh. She did not, but if she had, it would have been equally a laugh of nervous fear. She realized suddenly, with wonder: The Lizard's as scared as I am.

"Open for me, Kylis."

Incredulity was her first reaction. He would not joke, he could not, but he might mock her. Or was he asking her an impossibility, knowing she would refuse, so he could offer to let her alone if Gryf would return to the tetras? She kept her voice very calm.

"I can't do that."

"Don't you think I'm serious?"

"How could you be?"

He forced away his scowl, like an inexperienced mime changing expressions. The muscles of his jaw were set. He moved closer, so she had to look up to see his eyes.

"I am."

"But that's not something you ask for," Kylis said. "That's something a family all wants and decides on." She realized he would not understand what she meant.

"*I've* decided. There's only me now." His voice was only a bit too loud.

"Aren't you lonely?" She heard her words, not knowing why she had said them. If the Lizard had been hurt, she would revel in his pain. She could not imagine people who would live with him, unless something terrible had changed him.

"I had a kid—" He cut himself off, scowling, angry for revealing so much.

"Ah," she said involuntarily. She had seen

his manner of superficial control over badly suppressed violence before. Screwtop gave the Lizard justifiable opportunities to use his rage. Anywhere else it would burst out whenever he felt safe, against anyone who was defenseless and vulnerable. This was the kind of person who was asking her for a child.

"The board had no right to give him to her instead of me."

He would think that, of course. No right to protect the child? She did not say it.

"Well?"

To comply would be easy. She would probably be allowed to live in the comfort and coolness of the domes, and of course she would get good food. She could forget the dangerous machines and the Lizard's whip. She imagined what it would be like to feel a child quickening within her, and she imagined waiting to give birth to a human being, knowing she must hand it over to the Lizard to raise, all alone, with no other model, no other teacher, only this dreadful, crippled person.

"No," she said.

"You could if you wanted to."

So many things she had discovered about herself here had mocked her; now it was a claim she had once made to Gryf: I would do anything to get out of here.

"Leave it at that," she said quietly. "I don't want to." She backed away.

"I thought you were stubborn and strong. Maybe I made a mistake. Maybe you're just stupid, or crazy like the rest of them."

She tried to think of words he would understand, but always came up against the irreconcilable differences between her perception of the Lizard and what he thought of himself. He would not recognize her description.

"Or you want something more from me. What is it?"

She started to say there was nothing, but hesitated. "All right," she said, afraid her voice would be too shrill. Somehow it sounded perfectly normal. "Tell Gryf's people to set him free. Get Jason a parole and a ticket off-world." For a moment she almost allowed herself to hope he had believed her offer was sincere. She was a very good liar.

The Lizard's expression changed. "No. I need them around so you'll do what I say."

"I won't."

"Pick something else."

For an instant's flash Kylis remembered being taunted like this before, when she was very small. Anything but that. Anything but what you really want. She pushed the recollection away.

"There isn't anything else," she said.

"Don't hold out. You can't bribe me to let them go. I'm not a fool."

He needed no officially acceptable reason to hurt her. She knew that. Fear of his kind of power was almost an instinctive reaction for Kylis. But she whispered, "Yes, Lizard, you are," and, half blind, she turned and fled.

She almost outran him, but he lunged, grabbed her shoulder, pulled her around. "Kylis—"

Standing stiffly, coldly, she looked at his hand. "If that's what you want—"

Even the Lizard was not that twisted. Slowly, he let his hand fall to his side.

"I could force you," he said.

Her gaze met his and did not waver. "Could you?"

"I could drug you."

"For seven sets?" She realized, with a jog of alienness, that she had unconsciously translated the time from standard months to sets of forty days.

"Long enough to mess up your control. Long enough to make you pregnant."

"You couldn't keep me alive that long, drugged down that far. If the drugs didn't kill it, I would. I wouldn't even need to be conscious. I could abort it."

"I don't think you're that good."

"I am. You can't live like I did and not be that good."

"I can put you in the deprivation box until you swear to—"

She laughed bitterly. "And expect me to honor that oath?"

"You'd have children with Gryf and Jason."

This was real, much more than a game for the Lizard to play against Gryf. He wanted her compliance desperately. Kylis was certain of that, as certain as she was that he would use his own dreams to help fulfill his duty to Redsun. Still she could not understand why he felt he had some right to accuse her.

"Not like this," she said. "*With* them—but

not *for* one of them. And they wouldn't make themselves fertile, either, if you were a woman and asked one of them to give you a child."

"I'm quitting. I'd take him out of here. I'd give him a good home. Am I asking that much? I'm offering a lot for a little of your time and one ovulation." His voice held the roughness of rising temper.

"You're asking for a human being."

She waited for some reaction, any reaction, but he just stood there, accepting what she said as a simple statement of fact without emotional meaning or moral resonance.

"I'd kill a child before I'd give it to you," she said. "I'd kill myself." She felt herself trembling, though it did not show in her hands or in her voice. She was trembling because what she had said was true.

He reacted not at all. She turned and ran into the darkness, and this time the Lizard did not follow.

When she was sure she was not being watched, she returned to Gryf's rock in the forest. Gryf still slept. He had not moved from the time he fell asleep, but the gray rock around him gleamed with his sweat. Kylis sat down beside him, drew up her knees and wrapped her arms around them, put her head down. She had never felt as she felt now—unclean by implication, ashamed, diminished—and she could not explain the feeling to herself. She felt a tear slide down her cheek and clenched her teeth in anger. He will not make me cry, she thought. She breathed deeply, slowly, thinking, Control.

Slow the heartbeat, turn off the adrenaline, you don't need it now. Relax. Her body, at least, responded. Kylis sat motionless for a long time.

The heavy, moist wind began to blow, bringing low black clouds to cut off the stars. Soon it would be too dark to see.

"Gryf?" Kylis touched his shoulder. He did not move until she shook him gently; then he woke with a start.

"Storm's coming," Kylis said.

In the dimming starlight, a blond lock of Gryf's hair glinted as he rose. Kylis helped him up. Dead ferns rustled at their feet, and the sleeping insects wrapped themselves more closely in their wings.

At the edge of the forest Kylis and Gryf picked their way across a slag heap and reached the trail to the prisoners' area. A faint blue glow emanated from their shelter, where Jason sat hunched over a cold light reading a book he had managed to scrounge. He did not hear them until they climbed the stairs.

"I was beginning to get worried," he said mildly, squinting to see them past the light.

"Gryf was sick."

"You okay now?" Jason asked.

Gryf nodded, and he and Kylis sat down in the circle of bioluminescence that did not waver in the wind. Jason put his book away and got their rations and water bottles from the locker. The stalks Kylis had picked were by now a bit wilted, but she gave them to Gryf anyway. He shared them out. The meal was slightly better and slightly more pleasant than most at Screwtop, but Kylis was not hungry. She was ashamed to tell her friends what had happened.

"What's the matter?" Jason asked suddenly.

"What?" Kylis glanced up at him, then at Gryf. Both were watching her with concern.

"You look upset."

"I'm okay." She leaned back gradually as she spoke, so her face was no longer in the light. "I'm tired, I guess." She searched for words to put into the silence. "I'm so tired I almost forgot to tell you we're all on night shift."

That was good enough news to change the subject and take her friends' attention from her. It was even good enough news to cheer her.

Later they returned to the hiding place in the forest and slept, lying close with Gryf in the middle. In the distance the sky flashed bright, then darkened. Only a faint mutter reached them, but the lightning revealed heavy clouds and the wind carried the sound closer. Kylis touched Gryf gently, taking comfort in his deep and regular breathing. Lightning scarred the sky again, and seconds later thunder rumbled softly. The wind rustled dry fronds.

Gryf stroked Kylis' tattooed shoulder. He touched her hand and their fingers intertwined.

"I wish you could get out," she whispered. "I wish you would." The lightning flashed again, vivid and close, its thunder simultaneous. Jason started in his sleep. During the brief flare Gryf looked at Kylis, frowning.

It began to rain.

In the morning Kylis woke by reflex, despite the absence of the siren. The whole day was free, but she and her friends had to rest, for the night shift was first on duty.

Gryf was already sitting up. He smiled in his it's-all-right way.

"Let's see," Kylis said.

He turned. The welts were silver-gray down their lengths, even where they crossed. They were uninfected and the ends had begun to heal. Gryf stretched his arms and looked over his shoulder. Kylis watched his face, the fine lines at the corners of his eyes, but he did not flinch. Biocontrol was one thing Kylis had proper training in, and she knew Gryf could not stretch human limits indefinitely. This time, though, he had succeeded.

"How much better are you?" she asked.

He grinned and Kylis laughed in spite of herself. She forced away the thought and worry of the Lizard. Together she and Gryf woke Jason.

But all the rest of the day her apprehension grew. She was certain the Lizard would not accept her refusal easily. Now Kylis had to look twice at the little movements in her peripheral vision, once to make sure they were not hallucinations and again to make sure they were not the Lizard. By evening she was taut with acting out a pose of normality and maintaining an artificial calm, and she was affecting Jason and Gryf with

her agitation. She would not speak of the
reason. She could be nearly as stubborn as
Gryf.

Kylis was almost relieved when the siren
shrieked and they had to return to the in-
stallation to gather their rations and the set's
allowance of medicinal soap. She had tried
being angry, and sullen, and heedless, but
under it all she was frightened.

They walked past the guard stations,
across the lengthening shadows of afternoon. At the top of the Pit they stopped, looking down. But they could not delay; they
descended.

The heat from the unworked day seemed
to pool in the center of Screwtop. The sides
of the Pit reflected heat; the metal of the
machinery radiated it. The effects of temperature and noise combined synergistically.

Kylis and Gryf and Jason were all assigned to the probe crew. Across the Pit,
Kylis saw the Lizard watching her with no
expression at all. She looked away. Miria was
on this shift, too, but Kylis did not see her.

They dragged out the new drill bit and
raised it; it hung suspended above the shaft,
taller than a person, narrow and dangerous.
It frequently seemed to recognize the ab-
surdity of its domestication by weak human
beings, and rebelled. At Screwtop it was all
too easy to ascribe personality and malevo-
lent intentions to inanimate objects.

Shaft sections lay in racks like giant petals
around the stem of the drill, fanning out in
rays opposite the bubble-covered works of
the first two generators. The hum of turbines

spread across the floor of the Pit, through bootsoles, reaching flesh and blood and bone. To Kylis, the vibration seemed to be the anger of the wounded earth, unwillingly giving up the secrets and the energy of its interior, helpless in its resentment.

When this shaft was finished, the temperature at its bottom would approach 800 degrees C. When the crew broke through the caprock and released the pressure, that temperature was enough to turn the water below into superheated steam. It was enough to drive another generator. It was enough, if they did not seal the caprock properly, to kill them all instantly. They would seal it, tap it, and build an air-conditioned bubble over it. Then engineers, heavily protected, would move in and build the machinery. The prisoners, who were not trusted anywhere near the generators, would move farther on to drill another well.

This was a clean way of generating power, and cheap in all but human terms. The wells eventually ran dry and power needs for North Continent grew greater. Redsun had no fossil fuel, few radioactive elements, too many clouds to use the energy of its dim star.

Gryf's job was to guide the shaft sections to the drill. Some concession was made to his value; he was not put on the most dangerous jobs. The command to begin was given, and the small contrived delays and grumblings ceased.

The work turned the prisoners almost into automata. It was monotonous, but not monotonous enough. Complete boredom would

have allowed daydreams, but danger hung
too close for fantasies. Sweat slid into Kylis'
eyes when she was too busy to wipe it away.
The world sparkled and stung around her.
The night passed slowly. The Lizard watched
from a distance, a shade like any other
shadow. While he was near, Kylis felt alone
and, somehow, obscenely naked.

At midnight the prisoners were allowed to
stop for a few minutes to eat. Gryf eased
himself down the control tower ladder. At the
bottom, Kylis and Jason waited for him.
They sat together to eat and swallow salt
tablets. The break gave them time to rest
against the morning.

Kylis sat on the ground, her back against
metal, half asleep, waiting for the bell. The
floor of the Pit was wet and muddy and lit-
tered with broken rock and ash, so she did
not lie down. The Lizard had kept his distance all evening. Kylis thought he was unlikely to do anything direct while she was
among so many people, though they could do
nothing against him.

"Get up."

She started, frightened out of a light doze
by the Lizard's voice. He and his people had
their backs to her; they moved between her
and Gryf and encircled him. He rose, emerg-
ing from the shadows like a tortoiseshell cat.

The Lizard looked at him, then at Kylis.
"Take him," he said to his people.

"What are you going to do?" Hearing the
note of panic in her own voice, Kylis
clenched her fists.

"The tetras want him back. They need him. They're getting impatient."

"You're sending him home?" Kylis asked in disbelief.

"Of course," the Lizard said. He looked away from Kylis, at Gryf. "As soon as he's had enough of the deprivation box."

Beside Gryf, Jason stood up. Gryf put his hand on Jason's arm. The Lizard's people were moving nearer, closing in, should the Lizard need aid. A few of the prisoners came closer to see what was happening. Miria was among them. Kylis watched her from shadows, unseen. As the guards led Gryf away, Miria half smiled. Kylis wanted to scream with rage.

"How will they like it if you kill him?" Jason shouted.

"They take that chance," the Lizard said.

"It won't work," Kylis said. The deprivation box would never make Gryf go back to the tetras, and it could not force Kylis to do what the Lizard wanted. Even for Gryf she could not do that.

"Won't it?" The Lizard's voice was heavy and angry.

"Don't do this to him," Kylis said. "Gryf is—just being here is like being in the box. If you put him in a real one—" She was pleading for Gryf; she had never begged for anything in her life. The worst of it was she knew it was useless. She hoped bitterly that Miria was still human enough to understand what her spying had done.

"Shall I take you instead of him?" Without

waiting for an answer, laughing at her, the
Lizard turned away.

"Yes," Kylis said.

He swung around, astonished.

"You can put me in the box instead of
him."

The Lizard sneered at her. "And send the
tetras you instead of him? What use do you
think you'd be to any of *them*? You could be
a pet—you could be a host mother for another little speckled baby!"

Leaning down, scooping up a handful of
mud, Kylis took one step toward the Lizard
and threw the sticky clay. It caught him in
the chest, spattering his black uniform and
pale skin. Kylis turned, bending down again.
This time the clay was heavy and rocky.

"Kylis!" Jason cried.

"And *you*!" Kylis shouted. She flung the
mud and stones at Miria.

As the Lizard's people grabbed her, Kylis
saw Miria fall. Under the spotlights the clay
was red, but not as red as the blood spurting
from Miria's forehead.

The Lizard, scowling, wiping clay from his
chin, barely glanced at Miria's unmoving
form. He gestured to Kylis.

"Put her where she can't hurt anyone
else."

They marched her away, leaving Jason behind, alone.

They put Kylis in a bare cell with one glass
wall and a ledge without corners and venti-
lation that did not temper the heat. They
stripped her and locked her in. The room

passively prevented self-injury; even the walls and the window yielded softly to blows.

From inside, she could see the deprivation box. It was the correct shape for a coffin, but larger, and it stood on supports that eliminated the vibration of the generator.

The guards led Gryf into the deprivation room. He, too, was naked, and the guards had hosed him down. He looked around quickly, like a hunted animal alarmed from two sides at once. There was no help, only Kylis, pressed against the window with her fists clenched. Gryf tried to smile, but she could see he was afraid.

As they blindfolded him and worked to prepare him, Kylis remembered the feel of the soft padding packed in around her body, restraining head and arms and legs, preventing all movement and all sensation. First it had been pleasant; the box was dark and silent and gave no sensation of either heat or cold. Tubes and painless needles carried wastes from her body and nourishment in. Kylis had slept for what seemed a very long time, until her body became saturated with sleep. Without any tactile stimulation she grew remote from the physical world, and shrank down as a being to a small spot of consciousness behind the place her eyes had been. She then tried to put herself in a trance, but they had expected that. They prevented it with drugs. Her thoughts had become knit with fantasies, at first such gentle ones that she did not notice. Later they separated themselves from reality and became bizarre and identifiable. Finally they were indistinguishable from a reality too remote to believe in. She remembered the encompassing certainty of madness.

Kylis watched them lock Gryf into the same fate. They turned on the monitors. If he tried to ask to be let out, the subvocalization would be detected and his wish would be granted.

After that no one came near them. Kylis' sentence in the box had been eight days, but the sensory deprivation had overcome her time sense and stretched the time to weeks, months, years. She spent her time now waiting, almost as isolated. At intervals she fell asleep without meaning to, but when she awoke, everything was always the same. She was afraid to think of Gryf, afraid to think what might be happening to Jason alone outside, afraid to think about herself. The hallucinations crept back to haunt her. The glass turned to ice and melted in puddles, and the walls turned to snow clouds and drifted away. Her body would begin to shiver, and then she would realize that the walls were still there, quite real, and she would feel the heat again. She would feel Gryf's touch, and turn to embrace him, but he was never there. She felt herself slipping into a pit of confusion and visions and she could not gather strength or will to pull herself out. Sometimes she cried.

She lay in the cell and felt herself change, felt her courage dissolve in the sterile whiteness. The floor of the cell cradled her, softly, like a soothing voice telling her she could do what was easiest, anything that would ensure her own survival.

She sat up abruptly, digging her nails into her palms.

If she believed all that, she should yell and beat her fists on the glass until the guards came, beg them to take her to the Lizard, and do what he had asked. If she did that, everything Gryf was going through and everything she had endured would be betrayed. If she decided now to let another person make her decisions for her, or if she lost herself so completely that she could not make them herself, then she had only trivial reasons for what she had done.

Her reasons were not trivial; she could not force herself to believe they were, not for Gryf's sake or Jason's or her own. Gryf had found the strength to gamble coming to Screwtop on the chance of his own freedom; Jason had found the strength to stay alive where by all rights he should have died. Kylis knew she would have to find the same kind of strength to keep her sanity and her control.

She wiped the back of her hand across her eyes, put her right hand on the point of her left shoulder, leaned against the wall, and very slowly relaxed, concentrating on the reality of each individual muscle, the touch of plastic beneath her, the drop of sweat sliding down between her breasts.

When a cool draft of air brushed her legs, she opened her eyes. The Lizard stood in the doorway, looking down at her, a black shape surrounded by concentric rings of color. She had never seen him with such a gentle expression, but she did not return his expectant smile.

"Have you decided?"

Kylis blinked and all the bright colors dispersed, leaving a stark black-clothed figure. His expression hardened as Kylis gradually returned to Redsun's hell and made the connections she needed to answer him. Her fingers were half curled. She turned her hands over and flattened them on the floor.

"You haven't changed . . . you haven't changed me."

The Lizard glared at her, his expression changing to disbelief. Kylis said nothing more. She did not move. The Lizard made a sound of disgust and slammed the door. The cool air stopped.

He did not return, but Kylis did not try to convince herself she had beaten him.

She stared through the window and willed the tetras to come and free her friend. They must keep track of what was done to him. She could not believe they did not realize what such isolation would do to one of their own kind.

She had been staring at the same scene for so long that it took her a moment to realize it had changed. Four guards came in and began to open the sensory deprivation chamber. Kylis leaped up and pressed her hands to the glass. The deprivation chamber swung open. Kylis remembered her own first glimpse of light as the guards had pulled the padding from her eyes and disconnected tubes and needles. Gryf would be trying to focus his black-flecked blue eyes, blinking; his roan eyelashes would brush his cheeks.

The guards lifted him out, and he did not move. His long limbs dangled limp and lifeless. They carried him away.

Kylis sank to the floor and hugged her knees, hiding her face. When the guards came, they had to pull her to her feet and shake and slap her to force her to stand. They led her through their compound and pushed her through the exit, locking the gate behind her. They did not speak.

Kylis stood in the harsh illumination of spotlights for a few blank moments, then walked slowly toward the comforting shadows of night. She had needed darkness for a long time. Everything seemed more than real, with the absurd clarity of shock.

She saw Jason before he heard her; he was a pale patch on the edge of the light, sitting with his knees drawn up and his head down. Kylis was afraid to go to him.

"Kylis?"

She stopped. Jason's voice was rough, almost controlled but breaking. She turned around and saw him peering at her over his folded arms. His eyes were very bright. He pushed himself to his feet.

"I was afraid," he said. "I was afraid they'd take you both, and I didn't want to stay here alone."

"Go away."

"What? Kylis, why?"

"Gryf's dead." Desperation made her cruel. She wanted to go to him, and mourn with him, but she was afraid she would cause his destruction too. "And Gryf's the only thing that kept us together."

Stunned, Jason said nothing.

"Stay away from me," Kylis said, and walked past him.

"If Gryf is dead, we've got to—"

"No!"

"Are you sure he's dead? What happened?"

"I'm sure." She did not face him.

He put his hands on her shoulders. "We've got to get out of here before they kill us too. We've got to get north and tell people what's going on."

"Crazy!" She pulled free.

"Don't do this to me, Kylis."

His plea sliced through her grief and guilt, and even through her fear for him. She could not stand to hurt him. There was no fault in Jason, and no blame to assign to him. His only flaw was a loyalty she hardly deserved. Kylis looked around her, at the bare earth and the distant machines and the soft black ferns, all so alien. She turned back.

"I'm sorry," she said.

They held each other, but it was not enough comfort. Jason's tears fell cool on her shoulder, but she could not cry.

"There's something more than Gryf and the tetras," Jason said. "Please let me help. Tell me why all this is happening."

She shook her head. "It's dangerous for you to stay with me."

Suddenly he clenched his fingers around her arm. She pulled back, startled, and when she looked up, he scared her. She had never seen cruelty in Jason, but that was how he looked, cruel and filled with hatred.

"Jason—"

"I won't kill him," he said. "I won't . . . let me go—" He looked down and realized he was gripping Kylis' arm. "Oh, gods." He let her go and turned and walked into the forest.

Rubbing the bruise he had left, Kylis slowly looked behind her. What Jason had seen was the Lizard watching them from the gateway of the guards' enclosure. He did not move. Kylis ran.

The thick band of multicolored stars, shining through breaks in the clouds, lighted the way only where the ferns did not close in overhead. Kylis stumbled through the darkness, not even slowing for pools of rainwater. Her legs ached from fighting the suction of wet clay. Suddenly her shoulder rammed a rough stalk and her momentum spun her, flinging her against another. She stopped, gasping for breath, the air burning her throat.

Kylis straightened and looked around, getting her bearings. The stars glittered like sparks in the surface of standing water. She walked more carefully among the ferns. Her footsteps spread ripples out around her and the water sloshed gently from her boots. Only when she reached the shelter of dead ferns did she realize how silly and unnecessary it had been for her to be careful not to fall.

Inside the cool nest she lay down and composed herself. When she finally caught her

breath, she began breathing slowly and reg-
ularly, counting her heartbeats. Gradually
she extended the number of beats for each
inhalation, for each exhalation, then she
slowed her heart as well. She thought about
Gryf, dying deliberately rather than giving
his life to those he hated. And she thought
about Jason, who would never kill even in
vengeance. She was certain of that. If she
were gone, he at least would be safe.

She felt the gasp reflex growing stronger
and set her perception of it aside. Her
breathing had ceased now, and her heartbeat
would stop soon. Her thoughts slowed, her
memory drifted to more pleasant times. She
found herself with Gryf again, kissing him,
standing in the clean hot lake, touched by
spray from the overflow pipe. She smiled. A
bright yellow star glittered through a gap between the ferns. Kylis let her eyes close,
shutting out the last light.

Insistent hands shook her. She was dimly
aware of them and of a voice calling her
name. She concentrated more strongly on
dying. A fist pounded her chest and she
gasped involuntarily. Someone leaned down
and breathed into her mouth, holding her
chin up and her head back, forcing air into
her lungs. Her heart pounded. Pushing the
person away, Kylis sat up angrily and almost
fainted.

Miria caught her and made her lie down
again. "Thank gods, I found you. I could hear
you but then you disappeared."

Kylis did not answer, but only blinked her

eyes against the light Miria carried. She tried to be angry at her, but it seemed too futile.

"Kylis!" Miria's voice rose in panic. "Are you there? Can you hear me?"

"Of course I'm here," she said. She felt dizzy. She wondered why Miria had asked such a silly question. "What do you mean, am I here?"

Miria relaxed and brightened her lantern. "I was afraid I'd come too late." She had a bad scar, pink and new, on her forehead.

"Get away from me. Why couldn't you let us alone?" Kylis knew she would not be able to try to kill herself again for quite a while; she had used up too much strength.

"Gryf's all right," Miria said.

Kylis stared at her. "But I saw— How do you know? You're lying!"

"He's all right, Kylis. I know. Please trust me."

"Trust you! You told the Lizard about Gryf and Jason and me! He never knew before how much he could hurt us! And now he'll go after Jason, too, so I'll—" She stopped.

"The Lizard knew you were together, but I never told him your plans. You honored me with a request to join your family. Do you think your judgment of me was so wrong?"

Kylis sighed. "It wasn't very good about the kid who turned me in." She had to rest and breathe a moment. "I saw you go inside the fence without any guards. And after that, the Lizard—"

"What was he trying to make you do?"

"Have a child and give it to him."

Miria sat back on her heels. "To *Lizard*?

Gods." She shook her head in disbelief, in
sympathy for Kylis, for anyone, particularly
a child who would come under the Lizard's
control. The yellow lantern glow glinted
from the dark and lighter brown strands of
Miria's hair. Kylis suddenly saw the two distinct colors for the first time. The lighter
brown was not sun streaked—it grew that
way naturally.

"You're a tetra, aren't you?"

Miria looked up, and Kylis knew she would
not lie. "Yes. Anyway," she said sadly, "I
used to be."

"They let you go?"

"No!" She ran her hand across her hair
and spoke more calmly. "No. I was never like
Gryf. I never understood what he wanted, at
least until a few days ago. After you and I
talked . . ." She drew in a long breath. "I was
in an accident. I was foolish. I took chances
I had no right to take, and I nearly drowned.
I died for several minutes. No oxygen could
get to my brain." She looked away, fiddling
with the control on the lantern. "I can remember who I used to be, but I'm not her
any more. I cannot do the work I was meant
for. I feel so *stupid*. . . . I was afraid you'd
done that to yourself, damaged your brain."

"I'm all right, Miria." Kylis pushed herself
up on her elbow, suspicion and anger forgotten for a moment. "They sent you here because you had an accident? I think that's
awful."

"They could have—they should have, for
what I did. But I'm here to watch Gryf."

"To protect him? And you let them put him in the box?"

"You know enough about Gryf to know . . ." Miria's voice faltered. "I was not here only to be sure he lived. I wanted to force him to go back to his team. I wanted him . . . to make up for my failure."

"Why should he be responsible?"

"Because we're the same."

"Miria, I don't understand."

"He had the same place I did, on a different team. For important projects we make two groups and keep them separate, so they will confirm each other's research or develop alternate lines. Gryf is my transbrother. That is what we call tetras with the same parents in opposite couples." She rubbed her tawny forearm. "He was never meant to be a trans, of course, but it made no difference for the work. I crippled my team—I felt I had to keep Gryf from crippling his. I felt responsible."

"What's going to happen now?"

"Now . . ." Miria grasped Kylis' hands. "I'm not a tetra any more, Kylis. I have no vote. But I have a say, and I will do my best to persuade them to set him free."

"Miria, if you can—"

"I may do no better than keep them from sending him back here."

"Why did you change your mind?"

"Because of what you told me. I thought about it all the time Gryf was in deprivation. What I was doing to him to force him to share my loyalties—I almost killed him! I allowed the Lizard to torture him. You knew better than I what that could mean."

"But he's all right—you said he's all right."

"He is," Miria said quickly. "He will be. He overcame the drugs and put himself in a deep trance. I haven't lied. But I had nothing to do with freeing him before he died. I understand now what happened. After two days I realized Gryf must be let go, but the Lizard would not come out and he would not reply to my messages. He hoped to break you to his will and Gryf to mine. When he could not—finally he was afraid to keep Gryf in there any longer." Her voice was strained. "I've caused you so much pain. I hope some day you will all be together, and happy, and will be able to forgive me."

"Miria, I wish—"

The roar of a plane drowned out her words. Kylis glanced up reflexively. In all the time she had been at Screwtop, she had never heard or seen a plane. The North Continent was too far away, and here there was no place to land.

"I've got to go. I shouldn't have left Gryf, but I had to talk to you." Miria helped Kylis to her feet and out of the shelter. Kylis accepted the help gratefully. She felt wobbly.

They waded through shimmering shadows as Miria's light swung on her hip.

"Kylis," Miria said slowly, "I don't know what will happen. I hope I can free Gryf. I will try to help you. And Jason. But the Lizard serves the government well. They may decide he was right and I wrong. Whatever happens will take time, and I may not be able to do anything at all. I don't want to deceive you."

"I understand." Jason was in no less danger now, nor was she. But at least Gryf was safe. For a few moments Kylis could set aside her fear in the joy that he was alive.

They entered the compound's long clearing and reached the path that led toward the prisoners' shelter. Kylis saw the vertical takeoff plane hanging in midair. It slowly lowered itself, straight down, until it was out of sight behind the bank. Its engines slowed, idling.

"I can't take you to your shelter," Miria said. "I'm sorry—"

"Can I come the rest of the way—just to be sure—?"

"Gryf will already be on the plane, Kylis. You wouldn't be allowed to see him."

"All right," she said reluctantly. "I can get back myself from here."

"Are you sure? Will you be all right?"

Kylis nodded. "For now."

"Yes ..." Miria shifted her weight back and forth, reluctant to leave her alone but anxious to meet the plane.

"Go *on*," Kylis said.

"Yes. I must ..." She hesitated a moment more, then leaned quickly forward and embraced Kylis. "This is such a terrible place," she whispered. "Somehow I'll change it." She turned abruptly and hurried away.

Miria walked silhouetted against the lights and lantern. Kylis watched her go. At least she could hope now. She realized she must find Jason and tell him everything, but most particularly that Gryf was alive and out of the prison. Perhaps to be free. Then he could contact Jason's family—

"Oh, gods," Kylis groaned. "Miria! Miria, wait!" She ran toward the enclosure, stumbling from exhaustion.

She reached the bank above the fence just as Miria put her palm against the lock. The gate swung open.

"Miria!" Kylis cried. She was afraid Miria would not hear her over the engines of the plane, now inside the enclosure. But she cried out once more, sliding down the hill, and Miria turned.

She met Kylis between the bank and the fence, taking her elbow to support her as she struggled for breath.

"Jason's family," Kylis said. "Redsun thinks he's just a transient but he's not. If his people knew he was here, they'd ransom him." She remembered most of Jason's name, his family name, and told it to Miria. "Can you tell them? Just send a message?"

Miria's eyes widened. "Is that who he is?"

Kylis nodded.

"It will have to be done carefully, to keep his identity a secret, but I can do that, Kylis, yes." Then she sobered. "You'll be alone—"

"I'm all right alone. I've always been alone before. I can protect myself, but I can't protect Jason from the Lizard. Will you do it? Will you promise?"

"I promise."

Kylis clasped Miria's hands for an instant and let her go. Miria went inside the enclosure and boarded the plane. The engines screamed, and the aircraft rose, sliding forward like a hovercraft through the gateway. Clear of the fence, it rose higher until it had cleared the height of the marsh plants. It accelerated straight north.

Kylis watched it until it was out of sight. She wished she had seen Gryf, but now she believed Miria; she could believe he was alive.

In the eerie gentle light of dawn, as Kylis started away, the harsh spotlights dimmed one by one.

'Hugo's a swordsman,' Richard told him. 'He's very good, Ginnie, when you see him tell him he was perfectly right about Lynch's right cut. It was very helpful last night.'

'I wish I could have seen it.'

'So do I. Most of them didn't know what was happening till it was over. Alec, don't you want to eat? Let's go.' Briskly he steered a way back onto the street, through the blood-flecked snow. Sam Bonner rolled boozily up and past them, forgetting his objective at the sight of the velvet-clad woman standing abandoned in the doorway.

'Ginnie, lass! How's the prettiest ass in Riverside?'

'Cold,' Ginnie Vandall snapped, 'you stupid sot.'

THE TOR DOUBLES
Tor is proud to bring you the best in science fiction's short novels. An amazing amount of particularly fine science fiction is written at a length just too short to put in a book by itself, so we're providing them two at a time.

The Tor Doubles will be both new stories and older ones, all carefully chosen. Whichever side you start with, you will be able to turn the book over and enjoy the other side just as much.

P. BURKE WAS UGLY AND UNHAPPY . . .

But Delphi was beautiful, and P. Burke made all her decisions.

"Don't worry about a thing. You'll have people behind you whose job it is to select the most worthy products for you to use. Your job is just to do as they say. They'll show you what outfits to wear to parties, what suncars and viewers to buy and so on. That's all you'll have to do."

Parties—clothes—suncars!

Delphi's pink mouth opens. In P. Burke's starved seventeen-year-old head the ethics of product sponsorship float far away.

"Now tell me in your own words what your job is, Delphi."

"Yes sir. I—I'm to go to parties and buy things and use them as they tell me, to help the people who work in factories."

"And what did I say was so important."

"Oh—I shouldn't let anybody know, about the things."

It's out into the world for Delphi now.

Also by James Tiptree, Jr.
published by Tor Books

BRIGHTNESS FALLS FROM THE AIR
CROWN OF STARS (hardcover)
THE STARRY RIFT

JAMES TIPTREE, JR.
THE GIRL WHO WAS PLUGGED IN

A TOM DOHERTY ASSOCIATES BOOK
NEW YORK

This is a work of fiction. All the characters and events portrayed in this book are fictitious, and any resemblance to real people or events is purely coincidental.

THE GIRL WHO WAS PLUGGED IN

Copyright © 1973 by James Tiptree, Jr.

Reprinted by permission of the Estate of Alice B. Sheldon, and the estate's agent, Virginia Kidd Literary Agency. All rights reserved, including the right to reproduce this book or portions thereof in any form.

A TOR Book
Published by Tom Doherty Associates, Inc.
49 West 24 Street
New York, NY 10010

Cover art by Peter Gudynas
ISBN: 0-812-54554-0   Can. ISBN: 0-812-55959-2

First Tor edition: April 1989

Printed in the United States of America

0 9 8 7 6 5 4 3 2 1

■ ■ ■

Listen, zombie. Believe me. What I could tell you—you with your silly hands leaking sweat on your growth-stocks portfolio. One-ten lousy hacks of AT&T on twenty-point margin and you think you're Evel Knievel. AT&T?— You doubleknit dummy, how I'd love to show you something.

Look, dead daddy, I'd say. See for instance that rotten girl?

In the crowd over there, that one gaping at her gods. One rotten girl in the city of the future. (That's what I said.) Watch.

She's jammed among bodies, craning and peering with her soul yearning out of her eyeballs. Love! Oo-ooh, love them! Her gods are coming out of a store called Body East. Three youngbloods, larking along loverly. Dressed like simple street-people but ... smashing. See their great eyes swivel above their nose-filters, their hands lift shyly, their inhumanly tender lips melt? The crowd moans. Love! This whole boiling megacity, this whole fun future world loves its gods.

You don't believe gods, dad? Wait. Whatever turns you on, there's a god in the future for you, custom-made. Listen to this mob. "I touched his foot! Ow-oow, I TOUCHED Him!"

Even the people in the GTX tower up there love the gods—in their own way and for their own reasons.

The funky girl on the street, she just loves. Grooving on their beautiful lives, their mysterioso problems. No one ever told her about mortals who love a god and end up as a tree or a sighing sound. In a million years it'd never occur to her that her gods might love her back.

She's squashed against the wall now as the godlings come by. They move in a clear space. A holocam bobs above but its shadow never falls on them. The store display screens are magically clear of bodies as the gods glance in and a beggar underfoot is suddenly alone. They give him a token. "Aaaaah!" goes the crowd.

Now one of them flashes some wild new kind of timer and they all trot to catch a shuttle, just like people. The shuttle stops for them—more magic. The crowd sighs, closing back. The gods are gone.

(In a room far from—but not unconnected to—the GTX tower a molecular flipflop closes too, and three account tapes spin.)

Our girl is still stuck by the wall while guards and holocam equipment pull away. The adoration's fading from her face. That's good, because now you can see she's the ugly of the world. A tall monument to pituitary dystrophy. No surgeon would touch her. When she smiles, her jaw—it's half purple—almost bites her left eye out. She's also quite young, but who could care?

The crowd is pushing her along now, treating you to glimpses of her jumbled torso, her mismatched legs. At the corner she strains to send one last fond spasm after the godlings' shuttle. Then her face reverts to its usual expression of dim pain and she lurches onto the moving walkway, stumbling into people. The walkway junctions with another. She crosses, trips and collides with the casualty rail. Finally she comes out into a little bare place called a park. The sportshow is working, a basketball game in 3-di is going on right overhead. But all she does is squeeze onto a bench and huddle there while a ghostly free-throw goes by her ear.

After that nothing at all happens except a few furtive hand-mouth gestures which don't even interest her bench-mates.

But you're curious about the city? So ordinary after all, in the FUTURE?

Ah, there's plenty to swing with here—and it's not all that *far* in the future, dad. But pass up the sci-fi stuff for now, like for instance the holovision technology that's put TV and radio in museums. Or the worldwide carrier field bouncing down from satellites, controlling communication and transport systems all over the globe. That was a spin-off from asteroid mining, pass it by. We're watching that girl.

I'll give you just one goodie. Maybe you noticed on the sportshow or the streets? No commercials. No ads.

That's right. NO ADS. An eyeballer for you.

Look around. Not a billboard, sign, slogan, jingle, sky-write, blurb, sublimflash, in this whole fun world. Brand names? Only in those ticky little peep-screens on the stores and you could hardly call that advertising. How does that finger you?

Think about it. That girl is still sitting there.

She's parked right under the base of the GTX tower as a matter of fact. Look way up and you can see the sparkles from the bubble on top, up there among the domes of godland. Inside that bubble is a boardroom. Neat bronze shield on the door: Global Transmissions Corporation—not that that means anything.

I happen to know there's six people in that room. Five of them technically male, and the sixth isn't easily thought of as a mother. They are absolutely unremarkable. Those faces were seen once at their nuptials and will show again in their obituaries and impress nobody either time. If you're looking for the secret Big Blue Meanies of the world, forget it. I know. Zen, do I know! Flesh? Power? Glory? You'd horrify them.

What they do like up there is to have things orderly, especially their communications. You could say they've dedicated their lives to that, to freeing the world from garble. Their nightmares are about hemorrhages of information; channels screwed up, plans misimplemented, garble creeping in. Their gigantic wealth only worries them, it keeps opening new vistas of disorder. Luxury? They wear what their tailors put on them, eat what their cooks serve them. See that old boy there—his name is Isham—he's sipping water and frowning as he listens to a databall. The water was prescribed by his medistaff. It tastes awful. The databall also contains a disquieting message about his son, Paul.

But it's time to go back down, far below to our girl. Look!

She's toppled over sprawling on the ground.

A tepid commotion ensues among the bystanders. The consensus is she's dead, which she disproves by bubbling a little. And presently she's taken away by one of the superb ambulances of the future which are a real improvement over ours when one happens to be around.

At the local bellevue the usual things are done by the usual team of clowns aided by a saintly mop-pusher. Our girl revives enough to answer the questionnaire without which you can't die, even in the future. Finally she's cast up, a pumped-out hulk on a cot in the long, dim ward.

Again nothing happens for a while except that her eyes leak a little from the understandable disappointment of finding herself still alive.

But somewhere one GTX computer has been tickling another, and toward midnight something does happen. First comes an at-

tendant who pulls screens around her. Then
a man in a business doublet comes daintily
down the ward. He motions the attendant to
strip off the sheet and go.

The groggy girl-brute heaves up, big hands
clutching at bodyparts you'd pay not to see.

"Burke? P. Burke, is that your name?"

"Y-yes." Croak. "Are you . . . policeman?"

"No. They'll be along shortly, I expect.
Public suicide's a felony."

". . . I'm sorry."

He has a 'corder in his hand. "No family,
right?"

"No."

"You're seventeen. One year city college.
What did you study?"

"La—languages."

"H'm. Say something."

Unintelligible rasp.

He studies her. Seen close, he's not so elegant. Errand-boy type.

"Why did you try to kill yourself?"

She stares at him with dead-rat dignity,
hauling up the gray sheet. Give him a point,
he doesn't ask twice.

"Tell me, did you see Breath this afternoon?"

Dead as she nearly is, that ghastly love-
look wells up. Breath is the three young gods,
a loser's cult. Give the man another point, he
interprets her expression.

"How would you like to meet them?"

The girl's eyes bug out grotesquely.

"I have a job for someone like you. It's
hard work. If you did well you'd be meeting
Breath and stars like that all the time."

Is he insane? She's deciding she really did die.

"But it means you never see anybody you know again. Never, *ever*. You will be legally dead. Even the police won't know. Do you want to try?"

It all has to be repeated while her great jaw slowly sets. *Show me the fire I walk through.* Finally P. Burke's prints are in his 'corder, the man holding up the big rancid girl-body without a sign of distaste. It makes you wonder what else he does.

And then—THE MAGIC. Sudden silent trot of litter-bearers tucking P. Burke into something quite different from a bellevue stretcher, the oiled slide into the daddy of all luxury ambulances—real flowers in that holder!—and the long jarless rush to nowhere. Nowhere is warm and gleaming and kind with nurses. (Where did you hear that money can't buy genuine kindness?) And clean clouds folding P. Burke into bewildered sleep.

. . . Sleep which merges into feedings and washings and more sleeps, into drowsy moments of afternoon where midnight should be, and gentle businesslike voices and friendly (but very few) faces, and endless painless hysposprays and peculiar numbnesses. And later comes the steadying rhythm of days and nights, and a quickening which P. Burke doesn't identify as health, but only knows that the fungus place in her armpit is gone. And then she's up and following those few new faces with growing trust, first tottering, then walking strongly, all bet-

ter now, clumping down the short hall to the
tests, tests, tests, and the other things.

And here is our girl, looking—

If possible, worse than before. (You
thought this was Cinderella transistorized?)

The disimprovement in her looks comes
from the electrode jacks peeping out of her
sparse hair, and there are other meldings of
flesh and metal. On the other hand, that col-
lar and spinal plate are really an asset; you
won't miss seeing that neck.

P. Burke is ready for training in her new
job.

The training takes place in her suite and
is exactly what you'd call a charm course.
How to walk, sit, eat, speak, blow her nose,
how to stumble, to urinate, to hiccup—
DELICIOUSLY. How to make each nose-blow
or shrug delightfully, subtly different from
any ever spooled before. As the man said, it's
hard work.

But P. Burke proves apt. Somewhere in
that horrible body is a gazelle, a houri who
would have been buried forever without this
crazy chance. See the ugly duckling go!

Only it isn't precisely P. Burke who's stepping, laughing, shaking out her shining hair.
How could it be? P. Burke is doing it all
right, but she's doing it through something.
The something is to all appearances a live
girl. (You were warned, this is the FUTURE.)

When they first open the big cryocase and
show her her new body she says just one
word. Staring, gulping, "How?"

Simple, really. Watch P. Burke in her sack
and scuffs stump down the hall beside Joe,

the man who supervises the technical part of her training. Joe doesn't mind P. Burke's looks, he hasn't noticed them. To Joe, system matrices are beautiful.

They go into a dim room containing a huge cabinet like a one-man sauna and a console for Joe. The room has a glass wall that's all dark now. And just for your information, the whole shebang is five hundred feet underground near what used to be Carbondale, Pa.

Joe opens the sauna-cabinet like a big clamshell standing on end with a lot of funny business inside. Our girl shucks her shift and walks into it bare, totally unembarrassed. *Eager.* She settles in face-forward, butting jacks into sockets. Joe closes it carefully onto her humpback. Clunk. She can't see in there or hear or move. She hates this minute. But how she loves what comes next!

Joe's at his console and the lights on the other side of the glass wall come up. A room is on the other side, all fluff and kicky bits, a girly bedroom. In the bed is a small mound of silk with a rope of yellow hair hanging out.

The sheet stirs and gets whammed back flat.

Sitting up in the bed is the darlingest girl child you've EVER seen. She quivers—porno for angels. She sticks both her little arms straight up, flips her hair, looks around full of sleepy pazazz. Then she can't resist rubbing her hands down over her minibreasts and belly. Because, you see, it's the godawful P. Burke who is sitting there hugging her perfect girl-body, looking at you out of delighted eyes.

Then the kitten hops out of bed and crashes flat on the floor.

From the sauna in the dim room comes a strangled noise. P. Burke, trying to rub her wired-up elbow, is suddenly smothered in *two* bodies, electrodes jerking in her flesh. Joe juggles inputs, crooning into his mike. The flurry passes; it's all right.

In the lighted room the elf gets up, casts a cute glare at the glass wall and goes into a transparent cubicle. A bathroom, what else? She's a live girl, and live girls have to go to the bathroom after a night's sleep even if their brains are in a sauna cabinet in the next room. And P. Burke isn't in that cabinet, she's in the bathroom. Perfectly simple, if you have the glue for that closed training circuit that's letting her run her neural system by remote control.

Now let's get one thing clear. P. Burke does not *feel* her brain is in the sauna room, she feels she's in that sweet little body. When you wash your hands, do you feel the water is running on your brain? Of course not. You feel the water on your hand, although the "feeling" is actually a potential-pattern flickering over the electrochemical jelly between your ears. And it's delivered there via the long circuits from your hands. Just so, P. Burke's brain in the cabinet feels the water on her hands in the bathroom. The fact that the signals have jumped across space on the way in makes no difference at all. If you want the jargon, it's known as eccentric projection or sensory reference and you've done it all your life. Clear?

Time to leave the honey-pot to her toilet training—she's made a booboo with the toothbrush, because P. Burke can't get used to what she sees in the mirror—

But wait, you say. Where did that girl-body come from?

P. Burke asks that too, dragging out the words.

"They grow 'em," Joe tells her. He couldn't care less about the flesh department. "PDs. Placental decanters. Modified embryos, see? Fit the control implants in later. Without a Remote Operator it's just a vegetable. Look at the feet—no callus at all." (He knows because they told him.)

"Oh . . . oh, she's incredible . . ."

"Yeah, a neat job. Want to try walking-talking mode today? You're coming on fast."

And she is. Joe's reports and the reports from the nurse and the doctor and style man go to a bushy man upstairs who is some kind of medical cybertech but mostly a project administrator. His reports in turn go—to the GTX boardroom? Certainly not, did you think this is a *big* thing? His reports just go up. The point is, they're green, very green. P. Burke promises well.

So the bushy man—Doctor Tesla—has procedures to initiate. The little kitten's dossier in the Central Data Bank, for instance. Purely routine. And the phase-in schedule which will put her on the scene. This is simple: a small exposure in an off-network holo-show.

Next he has to line out the event which will fund and target her. That takes budget meetings, clearances, coordinations. The Burke project begins to recruit and grow. And there's the messy business of the name, which always gives Doctor Tesla an acute pain in the bush.

The name comes out weird, when it's suddenly discovered that Burke's "P." stands for "Philadelphia." Philadelphia? The astrologer grooves on it. Joe thinks it would help identification. The semantics girl references *brotherly love, Liberty-Bell, main-line, low teratogenesis*, blah-blah. Nicknames Philly? Pala? Pooty? Delphi? Is it good, bad? Finally "Delphi" is gingerly declared goodo. ("Burke" is replaced by something nobody remembers.)

Coming along now. We're at the official checkout down in the underground suite, which is as far as the training circuits reach. The bushy Doctor Tesla is there, braced by two budgetary types and a quiet fatherly man whom he handles like hot plasma.

Joe swings the door wide and she steps shyly in.

Their little Delphi, fifteen and flawless.

Tesla introduces her around. She's child-solemn, a beautiful baby to whom something so wonderful has happened you can feel the tingles. She doesn't smile, she . . . brims. That brimming joy is all that shows of P. Burke, the forgotten hulk in the sauna next door. But P. Burke doesn't know she's alive—it's Delphi who lives, every warm inch of her.

One of the budget types lets go a libidinous snuffle and freezes. The fatherly man, whose name is Mr. Cantle, clears his throat.

"Well, young lady, are you ready to go to work?"

"Yes, sir," gravely from the elf.

"We'll see. Has anybody told you what you're going to do for us?"

"No, sir." Joe and Tesla exhale quietly.

"Good." He eyes her, probing for the blind brain in the room next door.

"Do you know what *advertising* is?"

He's talking dirty, hitting to shock. Delphi's eyes widen and her little chin goes up. Joe is in ecstasy at the complex expressions P. Burke is getting through. Mr. Cantle waits.

"It's, well, it's when they used to tell people to buy things." She swallows. "It's not allowed."

"That's right." Mr. Cantle leans back, grave. "Advertising as it used to be is against the law. A display other than the legitimate use of the product, intended to promote its sale. In former times every manufacturer was free to tout his wares any way, place or time he could afford. All the media and most of the landscape was taken up with extravagant competing displays. The thing became uneconomic. The public rebelled. Since the so-called Huckster Act, sellers have been restrained to, I quote, displays in or on the product itself, visible during its legitimate use or in on-premise sales." Mr. Cantle leans forward. "Now tell me, Delphi, why do people buy one product rather than another?"

"Well . . ." Enchanting puzzlement from Delphi. "They, um, they see them and like them, or they hear about them from some-body?" (Touch of P. Burke there; she didn't say, from a friend.)

"Partly. Why did *you* buy your particular body-lift?"

"I never had a body-lift, sir."

Mr. Cantle frowns; what gutters do they drag for these Remotes?

"Well, what brand of water do you drink?"

"Just what was in the faucet, sir," says Delphi humbly. "I—I did try to boil it—"

"Good God." He scowls; Tesla stiffens. "Well, what did you boil it in? A cooker?"

The shining yellow head nods.

"What *brand* of cooker did you buy?"

"I didn't buy it, sir," says frightened P. Burke through Delphi's lips. "But—I know the best kind! Ananga has a Burnbabi, I saw the name when she—"

"Exactly!" Cantle's fatherly beam comes back strong; the Burnbabi account is a strong one, too. "You saw Ananga using one so you thought it must be good, eh? And it is good or a great human being like Ananga wouldn't be using it. Absolutely right. And now, Delphi, you know what you're going to be doing for us. You're going to show some products. Doesn't sound very hard, does it?"

"Oh, no, sir . . ." Baffled child's stare; Joe gloats.

"And you must never, *never* tell anyone what you're doing." Cantle's eyes bore for the brain behind this seductive child.

"You're wondering why we ask you to do this, naturally. There's a very serious reason. All those products people use, foods and healthaids and cookers and cleaners and clothes and cars—they're all made by *people*. Somebody put in years of hard work designing and making them. A man comes up with a fine new idea for a better product. He has to get a factory and machinery, and hire workmen. Now. What happens if people have no way of hearing about his product? Word-of-mouth is far too slow and unreliable. Nobody might ever stumble onto his new product or find out how good it was, right? And then he and all the people who worked for him—they'd go bankrupt, right? So, Delphi, there has to be *some way* that large numbers of people can get a look at a good new product, right? How? By letting people see you using it. You're giving that man a chance."

Delphi's little head is nodding in happy relief.

"Yes, sir. I do see now—but sir, it seems so sensible, why don't they let you—"

Cantle smiles sadly.

"It's an overreaction, my dear. History goes by swings. People overreact and pass harsh unrealistic laws which attempt to stamp out an essential social process. When this happens, the people who understand have to carry on as best they can until the pendulum swings back." He sighs. "The Huckster Laws are bad, inhuman laws, Delphi, despite their good intent. If they were strictly observed they would wreak havoc. Our economy, our society would be cruelly destroyed. We'd be back in caves!" His inner fire is showing; if the Huckster Laws were strictly enforced he'd be back punching a databank.

"It's our duty, Delphi. Our solemn social duty. We are not breaking the law. You will be using the product. But people wouldn't understand, if they knew. They would become upset just as you did. So you must be very, very careful not to mention any of this to anybody."

(And somebody will be very, very carefully monitoring Delphi's speech circuits.)

"Now we're all straight, aren't we? Little Delphi here"—He is speaking to the invisible creature next door —"Little Delphi is going to live a wonderful, exciting life. She's going to be a girl people watch. And she's going to be using fine products people will be glad to know about and helping the good people who make them. Yours will be a genuine social contribution." He keys up his pitch; the creature in there must be older.

Delphi digests this with ravishing gravity.

"But sir, how do I—?"

"Don't worry about a thing. You'll have people behind you whose job it is to select the most worthy products for you to use. Your job is just to do as they say. They'll show you what outfits to wear to parties, what suncars and viewers to buy and so on. That's all you have to do."

Parties—clothes—suncars! Delphi's pink mouth opens. In P. Burke's starved seventeen-year-old head the ethics of product sponsorship float far away.

"Now tell me in your own words what your job is, Delphi."

"Yes sir. I—I'm to go to parties and buy things and use them as they tell me, to help the people who work in factories."

"And what did I say was so important?"

"Oh—I shouldn't let anybody know, about the things."

"Right." Mr. Cantle has another paragraph he uses when the subject shows, well, immaturity. But he can sense only eagerness here. Good. He doesn't really enjoy the other speech.

"It's a lucky girl who can have all the fun she wants while doing good for others, isn't it?" He beams around. There's a prompt shuffling of chairs. Clearly this one is go.

Joe leads her out, grinning. The poor fool thinks they're admiring her coordination.

It's out into the world for Delphi now, and at this point the up-channels get used. On the administrative side account schedules are opened, subprojects activated. On the technical side the reserved bandwidth is cleared. (That carrier field, remember?) A new name is waiting for Delphi, a name she'll never hear. It's a long string of binaries which have been quietly cycling in a GTX tank ever since a certain Beautiful Person didn't wake up.

The name winks out of cycle, dances from pulses into modulations of modulations, whizzes through phasing, and shoots into a giga-band beam racing up to a synchronous satellite poised over Guatemala. From there the beam pours twenty thousand miles back to earth again, forming an all-pervasive field of structured energics supplying tuned demand-points all over the CanAm quadrant.

With that field, if you have the right credit rating you can sit at a GTX console and operate an ore-extractor in Brazil. Or—if you have some simple credentials like being able to walk on water—you could shoot a spool into the network holocam shows running day and night in every home and dorm and rec. site. *Or* you could create a continent-wide traffic jam. Is it any wonder GTX guards those inputs like a sacred trust?

Delphi's "name" appears as a tiny analyzable nonredundancy in the flux, and she'd be very proud if she knew about it. It would strike P. Burke as magic; P. Burke never even understood robotcars. But Delphi is in no sense a robot. Call her a waldo if you must. The fact is she's just a girl, a real live girl with her brain in an unusual place. A simple real-time on-line system with plenty of bitrate—even as you and you.

The point of all this hardware, which isn't very much hardware in this society, is so Delphi can walk out of that underground suite, a mobile demand-point draining an omnipresent fieldform. And she does— eighty-nine pounds of tender girl flesh and blood with a few metallic components, stepping out into the sunlight to be taken to her new life. A girl with everything going for her including a meditech escort. Walking lovely, stopping to widen her eyes at the big antennae system overhead.

The mere fact that something called P. Burke is left behind down underground has no bearing at all. P. Burke is totally unselfaware and happy as a clam in its shell.

(Her bed has been moved into the waldo cabinet room now.) And P. Burke isn't in the cabinet; P. Burke is climbing out of an airvan in a fabulous Colorado beef preserve and her name is Delphi. Delphi is looking at live Charlais steers and live cottonwoods and aspens gold against the blue smog and stepping over live grass to be welcomed by the reserve super's wife.

The super's wife is looking forward to a visit from Delphi and her friends and by a happy coincidence there's a holocam outfit here doing a piece for the nature nuts.

You could write the script yourself now, while Delphi learns a few rules about structural interferences and how to handle the tiny time lag which results from the new forty-thousand-mile parenthesis in her nervous system. That's right—the people with the leased holocam rig naturally find the gold aspen shadows look a lot better on Delphi's flank than they do on a steer. And Delphi's face improves the mountains too, when you can see them. But the nature freaks aren't quite as joyful as you'd expect.

"See you in Barcelona, kitten," the head man says sourly as they pack up.

"Barcelona?" echoes Delphi with that charming little subliminal lag. She sees where his hand is and steps back.

"Cool, it's not her fault," another man says wearily. He knocks back his grizzled hair. "Maybe they'll leave in some of the gut."

Delphi watches them go off to load the spools on the GTX transport for processing. Her hand roves over the breast the man had

touched. Back under Carbondale, P. Burke
has discovered something new about her
Delphi-body.

About the difference between Delphi and
her own grim carcass.

She's always known Delphi has almost no
sense of taste or smell. They explained about
that: Only so much bandwidth. You don't
have to taste a suncar, do you? And the slight
overall dimness of Delphi's sense of touch—
she's familiar with that, too. Fabrics that
would prickle P. Burke's own hide feel like
a cool plastic film to Delphi.

But the blank spots. It took her a while to
notice them. Delphi doesn't have much privacy; investments of her size don't. So she's
slow about discovering there's certain defi-
nite places where her beastly P. Burke body
feels things that Delphi's dainty flesh does
not. H'mm! Channel space again, she
thinks—and forgets it in the pure bliss of being Delphi.

You ask how a girl could forget a thing
like that? Look. P. Burke is about as far as
you can get from the concept *girl*. She's a
female, yes—but for her, sex is a four-letter
word spelled P-A-I-N. She isn't quite a virgin.
You don't want the details, she'd been about
twelve and the freak-lovers were bombed
blind. When they came down they threw her
out with a small hole in her anatomy and a
mortal one elsewhere. She dragged off to buy
her first and last shot and she can still hear
the clerk's incredulous guffaws.

Do you see why Delphi grins, stretching
her delicious little numb body in the sun she

faintly feels? Beams, saying, "Please, I'm ready now."

Ready for what? For Barcelona like the sour man said, where his nature-thing is now making it strong in the amateur section of the Festival. A winner! Like he also said, a lot of strip-mines and dead fish have been scrubbed but who cares with Delphi's darling face so visible?

So it's time for Delphi's face and her other delectabilities to show on Barcelona's Playa Nueva. Which means switching her channel to the EurAf synchsat.

They ship her at night so the nanosecond transfer isn't even noticed by that insignificant part of Delphi that lives five hundred feet under Carbondale, so excited the nurse has to make sure she eats. The circuit switches while Delphi "sleeps," that is, while P. Burke is out of the waldo cabinet. The next time she plugs in to open Delphi's eyes it's no different—do you notice which relay boards your phone calls go through?

And now for the event that turns the sugar-cube from Colorado into the PRINCESS.

Literally true, he's a prince, or rather an Infante of an old Spanish line that got shined up in the Neomonarchy. He's also eighty-one, with a passion for birds—the kind you see in zoos. Now it suddenly turns out that he isn't poor at all. Quite the reverse; his old sister laughs in their tax lawyer's face and starts restoring the family hacienda while the Infante totters out to court Delphi. And little Delphi begins to live the life of the gods.

What do gods do? Well, everything beautiful. But (remember Mr. Cantle?) the main point is Things. Ever see a god empty-handed? You can't be a god without at least a magic girdle or an eight-legged horse. But in the old days some stone tablets or winged sandals or a chariot drawn by virgins would do a god for life. No more! Gods make it on novelty now. By Delphi's time the hunt for new god-gear is turning the earth and seas inside-out and sending frantic fingers to the stars. And what gods have, mortals desire.

So Delphi starts on a Euromarket shopping spree squired by her old Infante, thereby doing her bit to stave off social collapse.

Social what? Didn't you get it, when Mr. Cantle talked about a world where advertising is banned and fifteen billion consumers are glued to their holocam shows? One capricious self-powered god can wreck you.

Take the nose-filter massacre. Years, the industry sweated years to achieve an almost invisible enzymatic filter. So one day a couple of pop-gods show up wearing nose-filters like *big purple bats*. By the end of the week the world market is screaming for purple bats. Then it switched to bird-heads and skulls, but by the time the industry retooled the crazies had dropped bird-heads and gone to injection globes. Blood!

Multiply that by a million consumer industries and you can see why it's economic to have a few controllable gods. Especially with the beautiful hunk of space R&D the Peace Department laid out for and which the taxpayers are only too glad to have taken off their hands by an outfit like GTX which everybody knows is almost a public trust.

And so you—or rather, GTX—find a creature like P. Burke and give her Delphi. And Delphi helps keep things *orderly*, she does what you tell her to. Why? That's right, Mr. Cantle never finished his speech.

But here come the tests of Delphi's button-nose twinkling in the torrent of news and entertainment. And she's noticed. The feedback shows a flock of viewers turning up the amps when this country baby gets tangled in her new colloidal body-jewels. She registers at a couple of major scenes, too, and when the Infante gives her a suncar, little Delphi trying out suncars is a tiger. There's a solid response in high-credit country. Mr. Cantle is humming his happy tune as he cancels a Benelux subnet option to guest her on a nude cook-show called Wok Venus.

And now for the superposh old-world wedding! The hacienda has Moorish baths and six-foot silver candelabras and real black horses and the Spanish Vatican blesses them. The final event is a grand gaucho ball with the old prince and his little Infanta on a bowered balcony. She's a spectacular doll of silver lace, wildly launching toy doves at her new friends whirling by below.

The Infante beams, twitches his old nose to the scent of her sweet excitement. His doctor has been very helpful. Surely now, after he has been so patient with the suncars and all the nonsense—

The child looks up at him, saying something incomprehensible about "breath." He makes out that she's complaining about the three singers she had begged for.

"They've changed!" she marvels. "Haven't they changed? They're so dreary. I'm so happy now!"

And Delphi falls fainting against a gothic vargueno.

Her American duenna rushes up, calls help. Delphi's eyes are open, but Delphi isn't there. The duenna pokes among Delphi's hair, slaps her. The old prince grimaces. He has no idea what she is beyond an excellent solution to his tax problems, but he had been a falconer in his youth. There comes to his mind the small pinioned birds which were flung up to stimulate the hawks. He pockets the veined claw to which he had promised certain indulgences and departs to design his new aviary.

And Delphi also departs with her retinue to the Infante's newly discovered yacht. The trouble isn't serious. It's only that five thousand miles away and five hundred feet down P. Burke has been doing it too well.

They've always known she has terrific aptitude. Joe says he never saw a Remote take over so fast. No disorientations, no rejections. The psychomed talks about self-alienation. She's going into Delphi like a salmon to the sea.

She isn't eating or sleeping, they can't keep her out of the body-cabinet to get her blood moving, there are necroses under her grisly sit-down. Crisis!

So Delphi gets a long "sleep" on the yacht and P. Burke gets it pounded through her perforated head that she's endangering Delphi. (Nurse Fleming thinks of that, thus alienating the psychomed.)

They rig a pool down there (Nurse Fleming again) and chase P. Burke back and forth. And she loves it. So naturally when they let her plug in again Delphi loves it too. Every noon beside the yacht's hydrofoils darling Delphi clips along in the blue sea they've warned her not to drink. And every night around the shoulder of the world an ill-shaped thing in a dark burrow beats its way across a sterile pool.

So presently the yacht stands up on its foils and carries Delphi to the program Mr. Cantle has waiting. It's long-range; she's scheduled for at least two decades' product life. Phase One calls for her to connect with a flock of young ultra-riches who are romping loose between Brioni and Djakarta where a competitor named PEV could pick them off.

A routine luxgear op, see; no politics, no policy angles, and the main budget items are the title and the yacht which was idle anyway. The storyline is that Delphi goes to accept some rare birds for her prince—who cares? The *point* is that the Haiti area is no longer radioactive and look!—the gods are there. And so are several new Carib West Happy Isles which can afford GTX rates, in fact two of them are GTX subsids.

But you don't want to get the idea that all these newsworthy people are wired-up robbies, for pity's sake. You don't need many if they're placed right. Delphi asks Joe about

that when he comes down to Baranquilla to
check her over. (P. Burke's own mouth hasn't
said much for a while.)

"Are there many like me?"

"Nobody's like you, buttons. Look, are you
still getting that Van Allen warble?"

"I mean, like Davy. Is he a Remote?"

(Davy is the lad who is helping her collect
the birds. A sincere redhead who needs a little more exposure.)

"Davy? He's one of Matt's boys, some psy-
chojob. They haven't any channel."

"What about the real ones? Djuma van O,
or Ali, or Jim Ten?"

"Djuma was born with a pile of GTX basic
where her brain should be, she's nothing but
a pain. Jimsy does what his astrologer tells
him. Look, peanut, where do you get the idea
you aren't real? You're the reallest. Aren't
you having joy?"

"Oh, Joe!" Flinging her little arms around
him and his analyzer grids. "Oh, *me gusto
mucho, muchissimo!*"

"Hey, hey." He pets her yellow head,
folding the analyzer.

Three thousand miles north and five hundred feet down a forgotten hulk in a body-
waldo glows.

And is she having joy. To waken out of the
nightmare of being P. Burke and find herself
a peri, a star-girl? On a yacht in paradise
with no more to do than adorn herself and
play with toys and attend revels and greet
her friends—her, P. Burke, having friends!—
and turn the right way for the holocams?
Joy!

And it shows. One look at Delphi and the viewers know: DREAMS CAN COME TRUE.

Look at her riding pillion on Davy's sea-bike, carrying an apoplectic macaw in a silver hoop. Oh, *Morton, let's go there this winter*! Or learning the Japanese chinchona from that Kobe group, in a dress that looks like a blowtorch rising from one knee, and which should sell big in Texas. *Morton, is that real fire?* Happy, happy little girl!

And Davy. He's her pet and her baby and she loves to help him fix his red-gold hair. (P. Burke marveling, running Delphi's fingers through the curls.) Of course Davy is one of Matt's boys—not impotent exactly, but very *very* low drive. (Nobody knows exactly what Matt does with his bitty budget but the boys are useful and one or two have made names.) He's perfect for Delphi; in fact the psychomed lets her take him to bed, two kittens in a basket. Davy doesn't mind the fact that Delphi "sleeps" like the dead. That's when P. Burke is out of the body-waldo up at Carbondale, attending to her own depressing needs.

A funny thing about that. Most of her sleepy-time Delphi's just a gently ticking lush little vegetable waiting for P. Burke to get back on the controls. But now and again Delphi all by herself smiles a bit or stirs in her "sleep." Once she breathed a sound: "Yes."

Under Carbondale P. Burke knows nothing. She's asleep too, dreaming of Delphi, what else? But if the bushy Dr. Tesla had heard that single syllable his bush would

have turned snow-white. Because Delphi is
TURNED OFF.

He doesn't. Davy is too dim to notice and
Delphi's staff boss, Hopkins, wasn't monitoring.

And they've all got something else to think
about now, because the cold-fire dress sells
half a million copies, and not only in Texas.
The GTX computers already know it. When
they correlate a minor demand for macaws
in Alaska the problem comes to human attention: Delphi is something special.

It's a problem, see, because Delphi is tar-
geted on a limited consumer bracket. Now it
turns out she has mass-pop potential—those
macaws in *Fairbanks*, man!—it's like trying
to shoot mice with an ABM. A whole new ball
game. Dr. Tesla and the fatherly Mr. Cantle
start going around in headquarters circles
and buddy-lunching together when they can
get away from a seventh-level weasel boy
who scares them both.

In the end it's decided to ship Delphi down
to the GTX holocam enclave in Chile to try a
spot on one of the mainstream shows. (Never
mind why an Infanta takes up acting.) The
holocam complex occupies a couple of
mountains where an observatory once used
the clear air. Holocam total-environment
shells are very expensive and electronically
super-stable. Inside them actors can move
freely without going off-register and the
whole scene or any selected part will show
up in the viewer's home in complete 3-di, so
real you can look up their noses and much
denser than you get from mobile rigs. You

can blow a tit ten feet tall when there's no molecular skiffle around.

The enclave looks—well, take everything you know about Hollywood-Burbank and throw it away. What Delphi sees coming down is a neat giant mushroom-farm, domes of all sizes up to monsters for the big games and stuff. It's orderly. The idea that art thrives on creative flamboyance has long been torpedoed by proof that what art needs is computers. Because this showbiz has something TV and Hollywood never had— *automated inbuilt viewer feedback*. Samples, ratings, critics, polls? Forget it. With that carrier field you can get real-time response-sensor readouts from every receiver in the world, served up at your console. That started as a thingie to give the public more influence on content.

Yes.

Try it, man. You're at the console. Slice to the sex-age-educ-econ-ethno-cetera audience of your choice and start. You can't miss. Where the feedback warms up, give 'em more of that. Warm—warmer—*hot*! You've hit it—the secret itch under those hides, the dream in those hearts. You don't need to know its name. With your hand controlling all the input and your eye reading all the response you can make them a god . . . and somebody'll do the same for you.

But Delphi just sees rainbows, when she gets through the degaussing ports and the field relay and takes her first look at the insides of those shells. The next thing she sees is a team of shapers and technicians de-

scending on her, and millisecond timers
everywhere. The tropical leisure is finished.
She's in gigabuck mainstream now, at the
funnel maw of the unceasing hose that's
pumping the sight and sound and flesh and
blood and sobs and laughs and dreams of *reality* into the world's happy head. Little Delphi is going plonk into a zillion homes in
prime time and nothing is left to chance.
Work!

And again Delphi proves apt. Of course it's
really P. Burke down under Carbondale
who's doing it, but who remembers that carcass? Certainly not P. Burke, she hasn't spoken through her own mouth for months.
Delphi doesn't even recall dreaming of her
when she wakes up.

As for the show itself, don't bother. It's
gone on so long no living soul could un-
scramble the plotline. Delphi's trial spot has
something to do with a widow and her dead
husband's brother's amnesia.

The flap comes after Delphi's spots begin
to flash out along the world-hose and the
feedback appears. You've guessed it, of
course. Sensational! As you'd say, they
IDENTIFY.

The report actually says something like
InskinEmp with a string of percentages
meaning that Delphi not only has it for anybody with a Y-chromosome, but also for
women and everything in between. It's the
sweet supernatural jackpot, the million-to-
one.

Remember your Harlow? A sexpot, sure.
But why did bitter hausfraus in Gary and

Memphis know that the vanilla-ice-cream goddess with the white hair and crazy eyebrows was *their baby girl*? And write loving letters to Jean warning her that their husbands weren't good enough for her? Why? The GTX analysts don't know either, but they know what to do with it when it happens.

(Back in his bird sanctuary the old Infante spots it without benefit of computers and gazes thoughtfully at his bride in widow's weeds. It might, he feels, be well to accelerate the completion of his studies.)

The excitement reaches down to the burrow under Carbondale where P. Burke gets two medical exams in a week and a chronically inflamed electrode is replaced. Nurse Fleming also gets an assistant who doesn't do much nursing but is very interested in access doors and identity tabs.

And in Chile little Delphi is promoted to a new home up among the stars' residential spreads and a private jitney to carry her to work. For Hopkins there's a new computer terminal and a full-time schedule man. What is the schedule crowded with?

Things.

And here begins the trouble. You probably saw that coming too.

"What does she think she is, a goddam *consumer rep*?" Mr. Cantle's fatherly face in Carbondale contorts.

"The girl's upset," Miss Fleming says stubbornly. "She believes that, what you told her about helping people and good new products."

"They are good products," Mr. Cantle snaps automatically, but his anger is under control. He hasn't got where he is by irrelevant reactions.

"She says the plastic gave her a rash and the glo-pills made her dizzy."

"Good god, she shouldn't swallow them," Doctor Tesla puts in agitatedly.

"You told her she'd use them," persists Miss Fleming.

Mr. Cantle is busy figuring how to ease this problem to the feral-faced young man. What, was it a goose that lays golden eggs?

Whatever he says to level Seven, down in Chile the offending products vanish. And a symbol goes into Delphi's tank matrix, one that means roughly *Balance unit resistance against PR index*. This means that Delphi's complaints will be endured as long as her Pop Response stays above a certain level. (What happens when it sinks need not concern us.) And to compensate, the price of her exposure-time rises again. She's a regular on the show now and response is still climbing.

See her under the sizzling lasers, in a holo-cam shell set up as a walkway accident. (The show is guesting an acupuncture school shill.)

"I don't think this new body-lift is safe," Delphi's saying. "It's made a funny blue spot on me—look, Mr. Vere."

She wiggles to show where the mini-grav pak that imparts a delicious sense of weightlessness is attached.

"So don't leave it *on*, Dee. With your

meat—watch that deck-spot, it's starting to synch."

"But if I don't wear it it isn't honest. They should insulate it more or something, don't you see?"

The show's beloved old father, who is the casualty, gives a senile snigger.

"I'll tell them," Mr. Vere mutters. "Look now, as you step back bend like this so it just shows, see? And hold two beats."

Obediently Delphi turns, and through the dazzle her eyes connect with a pair of strange dark ones. She squints. A quite young man is lounging alone by the port, apparently waiting to use the chamber.

Delphi's used by now to young men looking at her with many peculiar expressions, but she isn't used to what she gets here. A jolt of something somber and knowing. *Secrets.*

"Eyes! Eyes, Dee!"

She moves through the routine, stealing peeks at the stranger. He stares back. He knows something.

When they let her go she comes shyly to him.

"Living wild, kitten." Cool voice, hot underneath.

"What do you mean?"

"Dumping on the product. You trying to get dead?"

"But it isn't right," she tells him. "They don't know, but I do, I've been wearing it."

His cool is jolted.

"You're out of your head."

"Oh, they'll see I'm right when they check

it," she explains. "They're just so busy. When I tell them—"

He is staring down at little flower-face. His mouth opens, closes. "What are you doing in this sewer anyway? Who are you?"

Bewilderedly she says, "I'm Delphi."

"Holy Zen."

"What's wrong? Who are you, please?"

Her people are moving her out now, nodding at him.

"Sorry we ran over, Mister Uhunh," the script girl says.

He mutters something but it's lost as her convoy bustles her toward the flower-decked jitney.

(Hear the click of an invisible ignition-train being armed?)

"Who was he?" Delphi asks her hairman.

The hairman is bending up and down from his knees as he works.

"Paul. Isham. Three," he says and puts a comb in his mouth.

"Who's that? I can't see."

He mumbles around the comb, meaning "Are you jiving?" Because she has to be, in the middle of the GTX enclave.

Next day there's a darkly smoldering face under a turban-towel when Delphi and the show's paraplegic go to use the carbonated pool.

She looks.

He looks.

And the next day, too.

(Hear that automatic sequencer cutting in? The system couples, the fuels begin to travel.)

Poor old Isham senior. You have to feel

sorry for a man who values order: when he begets young, genetic information is still transmitted in the old ape way. One minute it's a happy midget with a rubber duck—look around and here's this huge healthy stranger, opaquely emotional, running with God knows who. Questions are heard where there's nothing to question, and eruptions claiming to be moral outrage. When this is called to Papa's attention—it may take time, in that boardroom—Papa does what he can, but without immortality-juice the problem is worrisome.

And young Paul Isham is a bear. He's bright and articulate and tender-souled and incessantly active and he and his friends are choking with appallment at the world their fathers made. And it hasn't taken Paul long to discover that *his* father's house has many mansions and even the GTX computers can't relate everything to everything else. He noses out a decaying project which adds up to something like, Sponsoring Marginal Creativity (the free-lance team that "discovered" Delphi was one such grantee). And from there it turns out that an agile lad named Isham can get his hands on a viable packet of GTX holocam facilities.

So here he is with his little band, way down the mushroom-farm mountain, busily spooling a show which has no relation to Delphi's. It's built on bizarre techniques and unsettling distortions pregnant with social protest. An *underground* expression to you.

All this isn't unknown to his father, of course, but so far it has done nothing more

than deepen Isham senior's apprehensive
frown.

Until Paul connects with Delphi.

And by the time Papa learns this, those invisible hypergolics have exploded, the energy-
shells are rushing out. For Paul, you see, is the
genuine article. He's serious. He dreams. He
even reads—for example, *Green Mansions*—
and he wept fiercely when those fiends burned
Rima alive.

When he hears that some new GTX pussy
is making it big he sneers and forgets it. He's
busy. He never connects the name with this
little girl making her idiotic, doomed protest
in the holocam chamber. This strangely simple little girl.

And she comes and looks up at him and he
sees Rima, lost Rima the enchanted bird girl,
and his unwired human heart goes twang.

And Rima turns out to be Delphi.

Do you need a map? The angry puzzlement.
The rejection of the dissonance Rima-hustling-
for-GTX-My-Father. Garbage, cannot be. The
loitering around the pool to confirm the
swindle ... dark eyes hitting on blue wonder, jerky words exchanged in a peculiar
stillness ... the dreadful reorganization of
the image into Rima-Delphi *in my Father's
tentacles*—

You don't need a map.

Nor for Delphi either, the girl who loved
her gods. She's seen their divine flesh close
now, heard their unamplified voices call her
name. She's played their god-games, worn
their garlands. She's even become a goddess
herself, though she doesn't believe it. She's

not disenchanted, don't think that. She's still full of love. It's just that some crazy kind of *hope* hasn't—

Really you can skip all this, when the loving little girl on the yellow-brick road meets a Man. A real human male burning with angry compassion and grandly concerned with human justice, who reaches for her with real male arms and—boom! She loves him back with all her heart.

A happy trip, see?

Except.

Except that it's really P. Burke five thousand miles away who loves Paul. P. Burke the monster down in a dungeon, smelling of electrode-paste. A caricature of a woman burning, melting, obsessed with true love. Trying over twenty-double-thousand miles of hard vacuum to reach her beloved through girl-flesh numbed by an invisible film. Feeling his arms around the body he thinks is hers, fighting through shadows to give herself to him. Trying to taste and smell him through beautiful dead nostrils, to love him back with a body that goes dead in the heart of the fire.

Perhaps you get P. Burke's state of mind?

She has phases. The trying, first. And the shame. The SHAME. *I am not what thou lovest.* And the fiercer trying. And the realization that there is no, no way, none. Never. *Never.* . . . A bit delayed, isn't it, her understanding that the bargain she made was forever? P. Burke should have noticed those stories about mortals who end up as grasshoppers.

You see the outcome—the funneling of all this agony into one dumb protoplasmic drive to fuse with Delphi. To leave, to close out the beast she is chained to. *To become Delphi*.

Of course it's impossible.

However her torments have an effect on Paul. Delphi-as-Rima is a potent enough love object, and liberating Delphi's mind requires hours of deeply satisfying instruction in the rottenness of it all. Add in Delphi's body worshipping his flesh, burning in the fire of P. Burke's savage heart—do you wonder Paul is involved?

That's not all.

By now they're spending every spare moment together and some that aren't so spare.

"Mister Isham, would you mind staying out of this sports sequence? The script calls for Davy here."

(Davy's still around, the exposure did him good.)

"What's the difference?" Paul yawns. "It's just an ad. I'm not blocking that thing."

Shocked silence at his two-letter word. The script girl swallows bravely.

"I'm sorry, sir, our directive is to do the *social sequence* exactly as scripted. We're having to respool the segments we did last week, Mister Hopkins is very angry with me."

"Who the hell is Hopkins? Where is he?"

"Oh, please, Paul. *Please*."

Paul unwraps himself, saunters back. The holocam crew nervously check their angles. The GTX boardroom has a foible about having things *pointed* at them and theirs. Cold shivers, when the image of an Isham nearly went onto the world beam beside that Diala-dinner.

Worse yet. Paul has no respect for the sacred schedules which are now a full-time job for ferret boy up at headquarters. Paul keeps forgetting to bring her back on time and poor Hopkins can't cope.

So pretty soon the boardroom data-ball has an urgent personal action-tab for Mr. Isham senior. They do it the gentle way, at first.

"I can't today, Paul."

"Why not?"

"They say I have to, it's *very* important."

He strokes the faint gold down on her narrow back. Under Carbondale, Pa., a blind mole-woman shivers.

"Important. Their importance. Making more gold. Can't you see? To them you're just a thing to get scratch with. A *huckster*. Are you going to let them screw you, Dee? Are you?"

"Oh, Paul—"

He doesn't know it but he's seeing a weirdie; Remotes aren't hooked up to flow tears.

"Just say no, Dee. No. Integrity. You have to."

"But they say, it's my job—"

"Will you believe I can take care of you, Dee? Baby, baby, you're letting them rip us. You have to choose. Tell them no."

"Paul . . . I w-will . . ."

And she does. Brave little Delphi (insane

P. Burke). Saying "No, please, I promised, Paul."

They try some more, still gently.

"Paul, Mr. Hopkins told me the reason they don't want us to be together so much. It's because of who you are, your father."

She thinks his father is like Mr. Cantle, maybe.

"Oh great. Hopkins. I'll fix him. Listen, I can't think about Hopkins now. Ken came back today, he found out something."

They are lying on the high Andes meadow watching his friends dive their singing kites.

"Would you believe, on the coast the police have *electrodes in their heads*?"

She stiffens in his arms.

"Yeah, weird. I thought they only used PP on criminals and the army. Don't you see, Dee—something has to be going on. Some movement. Maybe somebody's organizing. How can we find out?" He pounds the ground behind her. "We should make *contact*! If we could only find out."

"The, the news?" she asks distractedly.

"The news." He laughs. "There's nothing in the news except what they want people to know. Half the country could burn up and nobody would know it if they didn't want. Dee, can't you take what I'm explaining to you? They've got the whole world programmed! Total control of communication. They've got everybody's minds wired in to think what they show them and want what they give them and they give them what they're programmed to want—you can't break in or out of it, you can't get *hold* of it

anywhere. I don't think they even have a plan
except to keep things going round and
round—and God knows what's happening to
the people or the earth or the other planets,
maybe. One great big vortex of lies and garbage pouring round and round getting bigger and bigger and nothing can ever change.
If people don't wake up soon we're through!"

He pounds her stomach softly.

"You have to break out, Dee."

"I'll try, Paul, I will—"

"You're mine. They can't have you."

And he goes to see Hopkins, who is indeed
cowed.

But that night up under Carbondale the fatherly Mr. Cantle goes to see P. Burke.

P. Burke? On a cot in a utility robe like a
dead camel in a tent, she cannot at first com-
prehend that he is telling *her* to break it off
with Paul. P. Burke has never seen Paul. *Delphi* sees Paul. The fact is, P. Burke can no
longer clearly recall that she exists apart
from Delphi.

Mr. Cantle can scarcely believe it either
but he tries.

He points out the futility, the potential embarrassment for Paul. That gets a dim stare
from the bulk on the bed. Then he goes into
her duty to GTX, her job, isn't she grateful
for the opportunity, etcetera. He's very per-
suasive.

The cobwebby mouth of P. Burke opens
and croaks.

"No."

Nothing more seems to be forthcoming.

Mr. Cantle isn't dense, he knows an immovable obstacle when he bumps one. He also knows an irresistible force: GTX. The simple solution is to lock the waldo-cabinet until Paul gets tired of waiting for Delphi to wake up. But the cost, the schedules! And there's something odd here ... he eyes the corporate asset hulking on the bed and his hunch-sense prickles.

You see, Remotes don't love. They don't have real sex, the circuits designed that out from the start. So it's been assumed that it's *Paul* who is diverting himself or something with the pretty little body in Chile. P. Burke can only be doing what comes natural to any ambitious gutter-meat. It hasn't occurred to anyone that they're dealing with the real hairy thing whose shadow is blasting out of every holoshow on earth.

Love?

Mr. Cantle frowns. The idea is grotesque. But his instinct for the fuzzy line is strong; he will recommend flexibility.

And so, in Chile:

"Darling, I don't have to work tonight! And Friday too—isn't that right, Mr. Hopkins?"

"Oh, great. When does she come up for parole?"

"Mr. Isham, please be reasonable. Our schedule—surely your own production people must be needing you?"

This happens to be true. Paul goes away. Hopkins stares after him wondering distastefully why an Isham wants to ball a waldo. How sound are those boardroom belly-fears—garble creeps, creeps in! It never occurs to Hopkins that an Isham might not know what Delphi is.

Especially with Davy crying because Paul has kicked him out of Delphi's bed.

Delphi's bed is under a real window.

"Stars," Paul sleepily. He rolls over, pulling Delphi on top. "Are you aware that this is one of the last places on earth where people can see the stars? Tibet, too, maybe."

"Paul . . ."

"Go to sleep. I want to see you sleep."

"Paul, I . . . I sleep so *hard*, I mean, it's a joke how hard I am to wake up. Do you mind?"

"Yes."

But finally, fearfully, she must let go. So that five thousand miles north a crazy spent creature can crawl out to gulp concentrates and fall on her cot. But not for long. It's pink dawn when Delphi's eyes open to find Paul's arms around her, his voice saying rude, tender things. He's been kept awake. The nerveless little statue that was her Delphi-body nuzzled him in the night.

Insane hope rises, is fed a couple of nights later when he tells her she called his name in her sleep.

And that day Paul's arms keep her from work and Hopkins' wails go up to headquarters where the weasel-faced lad is working his sharp tailbone off packing Delphi's program. Mr. Cantle defuses that one. But next week it happens again, to a major client. And ferret-face has connections on the technical side.

Now you can see that when you have a field

of complexly heterodyned energy modulations tuned to a demand-point like Delphi
there are many problems of standwaves and
lash-back and skiffle of all sorts which are
normally balanced out with ease by the technology of the future. By the same token they
can be delicately unbalanced too, in ways
that feed back into the waldo operator with
striking results.

"Darling—what the hell! What's wrong?
DELPHI!"

Helpless shrieks, writhings. Then the
Rima-bird is lying wet and limp in his arms,
her eyes enormous.

"I . . . I wasn't supposed to . . ." she gasps
faintly, "They told me not to . . ."

"Oh my god—*Delphi*."

And his hard fingers are digging in her
thick yellow hair. Electronically knowledgeable fingers. They freeze.

"You're a *doll*! You're one of those. PP implants. They control you. I should have
known. Oh God, I should have known."

"No, Paul," she's sobbing. "No, no, no—"

"Damn them. Damn them, what they've
done—you're not *you*—"

He's shaking her, crouching over her in the
bed and jerking her back and forth, glaring
at the pitiful beauty.

"No!" She pleads (it's not true, that dark
bad dream back there). "I'm Delphi!"

"My father. Filth, pigs—damn them, damn
them, damn them."

"No, no," she babbles. "They were good to
me—" P. Burke underground mouthing,
"They were good to me—AAH-AAAAH!"

Another agony skewers her. Up north the sharp young man wants to make sure this so-tiny interference works. Paul can scarcely hang onto her, he's crying too. "I'll kill them."

His Delphi, a wired-up slave! Spikes in her brain, electronic shackles in his bird's heart. Remember when those savages burned Rima alive?

"I'll *kill* the man that's doing this to you."

He's still saying it afterward but she doesn't hear. She's sure he hates her now, all she wants is to die. When she finally understands that the fierceness is tenderness she thinks it's a miracle. *He knows—and he still loves!*

How can she guess that he's got it a little bit wrong?

You can't blame Paul. Give him credit that he's even heard about pleasure-pain implants and snoops, which by their nature aren't mentioned much by those who know them most intimately. That's what he thinks is being used on Delphi, something to *control* her. And to listen—he burns at the unknown ears in their bed.

Of waldo-bodies and objects like P. Burke he has heard nothing.

So it never crosses his mind as he looks down at his violated bird, sick with fury and love, that he isn't holding *all* of her. Do you need to be told the mad resolve jelling in him now?

To free Delphi.

How? Well, he is, after all, Paul Isham III.

And he even has an idea where the GTX neurolab is. In Carbondale.

But first things have to be done for Delphi, and for his own stomach. So he gives her back to Hopkins and departs in a restrained and discreet way. And the Chile staff is grateful and do not understand that his teeth don't normally show so much.

And a week passes in which Delphi is a very good, docile little ghost. They let her have the load of wildflowers Paul sends and the bland loving notes. (He's playing it coony.) And up in headquarters weasel boy feels that *his* destiny has clicked a notch onward and floats the word up that he's handy with little problems.

And no one knows what P. Burke thinks in any way whatever, except that Miss Fleming catches her flushing her food down the can and next night she faints in the pool. They haul her out and stick her with IVs. Miss Fleming frets, she's seen expressions like that before. But she wasn't around when crazies who called themselves Followers of the Fish looked through flames to life everlasting. P. Burke is seeing Heaven on the far side of death, too. Heaven is spelled P-a-u-l, but the idea's the same. *I will die and be born again in Delphi.*

Garbage, electronically speaking. No way.

Another week and Paul's madness has become a plan. (Remember, he does have friends.) He smolders, watching his love paraded by her masters. He turns out a scorching sequence for his own show. And finally, politely, he requests from Hopkins a morsel of his bird's free time, which duly arrives.

"I thought you didn't *want* me any more," she's repeating as they wing over mountain flanks in Paul's suncar. "Now you *know*—"

"Look at me!"

His hand covers her mouth and he's showing her a lettered card.

DON'T TALK THEY CAN HEAR EVERYTHING WE SAY.

I'M TAKING YOU AWAY NOW.

She kisses his hand. He nods urgently, flipping the card.

DON'T BE AFRAID. I CAN STOP THE PAIN IF THEY TRY TO HURT YOU.

With his free hand he shakes out a silvery scrambler-mesh on a power pack. She is dumbfounded.

THIS WILL CUT THE SIGNALS AND PROTECT YOU DARLING.

She's staring at him, her head going vaguely from side to side, No.

"Yes!" He grins triumphantly. "Yes!"

For a moment she wonders. That powered mesh will cut off the field, all right. It will also cut off Delphi. But he is *Paul*. Paul is kissing her, she can only seek him hungrily as he sweeps the suncar through a pass.

Ahead is an old jet ramp with a shiny bullet waiting to go. (Paul also has credits and a Name.) The little GTX patrol courier is built for nothing but speed. Paul and Delphi wedge in behind the pilot's extra fuel tank and there's no more talking when the torches start to scream.

They're screaming high over Quito before

Hopkins starts to worry. He wastes another hour tracking the beeper on Paul's suncar. The suncar is sailing a pattern out to sea. By the time they're sure it's empty and Hopkins gets on the hot flue to headquarters the fugitives are a sourceless howl above Carib West.

Up at headquarters weasel boy gets the squeal. His first impulse is to repeat his previous play but then his brain snaps to. This one is too hot. Because, see, although in the long run they can make P. Burke do anything at all except maybe *live*, instant emergencies can be tricky. And—Paul Isham III.

"Can't you order her back?"

They're all in the GTX tower monitor station, Mr. Cantle and ferret-face and Joe and a very neat man who is Mr. Isham senior's personal eyes and ears.

"No sir," Joe says doggedly. "We can read channels, particularly speech, but we can't interpolate organized pattern. It takes the waldo op to send one-to-one—"

"What are they saying?"

"Nothing at the moment, sir." The console jockey's eyes are closed. "I believe they are, ah, embracing."

"They're not answering," a traffic monitor says. "Still heading zero zero three zero—due north, sir."

"You're certain Kennedy is alerted not to fire on them?" the neat man asks anxiously.

"Yes sir."

"Can't you just turn her off?" The sharp-faced lad is angry. "Pull that pig out of the controls!"

"If you cut the transmission cold you'll kill the Remote," Joe explains for the third time. "Withdrawal has to be phased right, you have to fade over to the Remote's own autonomics. Heart, breathing, cerebellum would go blooey. If you pull Burke out you'll probably finish her too. It's a fantastic cybersystem, you don't want to do that."

"The investment." Mr. Cantle shudders.

Weasel boy puts his hand on the console jock's shoulder, it's the contact who arranged the No-no effect for him.

"We can at least give them a warning signal, sir." He licks his lips, gives the neat man his sweet ferret smile. "We know that does no damage."

Joe frowns, Mr. Cantle sighs. The neat man is murmuring into his wrist. He looks up. "I am authorized," he says reverently, "I am authorized to, ah, direct a signal. If this is the only course. But minimal, minimal."

Sharp-face squeezes his man's shoulder.

In the silver bullet shrieking over Charleston Paul feels Delphi arch in his arms. He reaches for the mesh, hot for action. She thrashes, pushing at his hands, her eyes roll. She's afraid of that mesh despite the agony. (And she's right.) Frantically Paul fights her in the cramped space, gets it over her head. As he turns the power up she burrows free under his arm and the spasm fades.

"They're calling you again, Mister Isham!" the pilot yells.

"Don't answer. Darling, keep this over your head damn it how can I—"

An AX90 barrels over their nose, there's a flash.

"Mister Isham! Those are Air Force jets!"

"Forget it," Paul shouts back. "They won't fire. Darling, don't be afraid."

Another AX90 rocks them.

"Would you mind pointing your pistol at my head where they can see it, sir?" the pilot howls.

Paul does so. The AX90s take up escort formation around them. The pilot goes back to figuring how he can collect from GTX too, and after Goldsboro AB the escort peels away.

"Holding the same course," Traffic is reporting to the group around the monitor. "Apparently they've taken on enough fuel to bring them to towerport here."

"In that case it's just a question of waiting for them to dock." Mr. Cantle's fatherly manner revives a bit.

"Why can't they cut off that damn freak's life-support," the sharp young man fumes. "It's ridiculous."

"They're working on it," Cantle assures him.

What they're doing, down under Carbondale, is arguing.

Miss Fleming's watchdog has summoned the bushy man to the waldo room.

"Miss Fleming, you will obey orders."

"You'll kill her if you try that, sir. I can't believe you meant it, that's why I didn't. We've already fed her enough sedative to affect heart action; if you cut any more oxygen she'll die in there."

The bushy man grimaces. "Get Doctor Quine here fast."

They wait, staring at the cabinet in which a drugged, ugly madwoman fights for consciousness, fights to hold Delphi's eyes open.

High over Richmond the silver pod starts a turn. Delphi is sagged into Paul's arm, her eyes swim up to him.

"Starting down now, baby. It'll be over soon, all you have to do is stay alive, Dee."

". . . Stay alive . . ."

The traffic monitor has caught them. "Sir! They've turned off for Carbondale—Control has contact—"

"Let's go."

But the headquarters posse is too late to intercept the courier wailing into Carbondale. And Paul's friends have come through again. The fugitives are out through the freight dock and into the neurolab admin port before the guard gets organized. At the elevator Paul's face plus his handgun get them in.

"I want Doctor—what's his name, Dee? Dee!"

". . . Tesla . . ." She's reeling on her feet.

"Doctor Tesla. Take me down to Tesla, fast."

Intercoms are squalling around them as they whoosh down, Paul's pistol in the guard's back. When the door slides open the bushy man is there.

"I'm Tesla."

"I'm Paul Isham. *Isham.* You're going to take your flaming implants out of this girl— now. Move!"

"What?"

"You heard me. Where's your operating room? Go!"

"But—"

"Move! Do I have to burn somebody?"

Paul waves the weapon at Dr. Quine, who has just appeared.

"No, no," says Tesla hurriedly. "But I can't, you know. It's impossible, there'll be nothing left."

"You screaming well can, right now. You mess up and I'll kill you," says Paul murderously. "Where is it, there? And wipe the feke that's on her circuits now."

He's backing them down the hall, Delphi heavy on his arm.

"Is this the place, baby? Where they did it to you?"

"Yes," she whispers, blinking at a door. "Yes . . ."

Because it is, see. Behind that door is the very suite where she was born.

Paul herds them through it into a gleaming hall. An inner door opens and a nurse and a gray man rush out. And freeze.

Paul sees there's something special about that inner door. He crowds them past it and pushes it open and looks in.

Inside is a big mean-looking cabinet with its front door panels ajar.

And inside that cabinet is a poisoned carcass to whom something wonderful, unspeakable, is happening. Inside is P. Burke the real living woman who knows that HE is there, coming closer—Paul whom she had fought to reach through forty thousand miles of ice—PAUL is here!—is yanking at the waldo doors—

The doors tear open and a monster rises up.

"Paul darling!" croaks the voice of love and the arms of love reach for him.

And he responds.

Wouldn't you, if a gaunt she-golem flab-naked and spouting wires and blood came at you clawing with metal studded paws—

"Get away!" He knocks wires.

It doesn't much matter which wires, P. Burke has so to speak her nervous system hanging out. Imagine somebody jerking a handful of your medulla—

She crashes onto the floor at his feet, flopping and roaring *"PAUL-PAUL-PAUL"* in rictus.

It's doubtful he recognizes his name or sees her life coming out of her eyes at him. And at the last it doesn't go to him. The eyes find Delphi, fainting by the doorway, and die.

Now of course Delphi is dead, too.

There's a total silence as Paul steps away from the thing by his foot.

"You killed her," Tesla says. "That was her."

"Your control." Paul is furious, the thought of that monster fastened into little Delphi's brain nauseates him. He sees her crumpling and holds out his arms. Not knowing she is dead.

And Delphi comes to him.

One foot before the other, not moving very well—but moving. Her darling face turns up. Paul is distracted by the terrible quiet, and when he looks down he sees only her tender little neck.

"Now you get the implants out," he warns them. Nobody moves.

"But, but she's dead," Miss Fleming whispers wildly.

Paul feels Delphi's life under his hand, they're talking about their monster. He aims his pistol at the gray man.

"You. If we aren't in your surgery when I count three I'm burning off this man's leg."

"Mr. Isham," Tesla says desperately, "you have just killed the person who animated the body you call Delphi. Delphi herself is dead. If you release your arm you'll see what I say is true."

The tone gets through. Slowly Paul opens his arm, looks down.

"Delphi?"

She totters, sways, stays upright. Her face comes slowly up.

"Paul . . ." Tiny voice.

"Your crotty tricks," Paul snarls at them. "Move!"

"Look at her eyes," Dr. Quine croaks.

They look. One of Delphi's pupils fills the iris, her lips writhe weirdly.

"Shock." Paul grabs her to him. "*Fix* her!" He yells at them, aiming at Tesla.

"For God's sake . . . bring it in the lab." Tesla quavers.

"Goodbye-bye," says Delphi clearly. They lurch down the hall, Paul carrying her, and meet a wave of people.

Headquarters has arrived.

Joe takes one look and dives for the waldo room, running into Paul's gun.

"Oh no, you don't."

Everybody is yelling. The little thing in his arm stirs, says plaintively, "I'm Delphi."

And all through the ensuing jabber and ranting she hangs on, keeping it up, the ghost of P. Burke or whatever whispering crazily "Paul . . . Paul . . . Please, I'm Delphi . . . Paul?"

"I'm here, darling, I'm here." He's holding her in the nursing bed. Tesla talks, talks, talks unheard.

"Paul . . . don't sleep . . ." The ghost-voice whispers. Paul is in agony, he will not accept, WILL NOT believe.

Tesla runs down.

And then near midnight Delphi says roughly, "Ag-ag-ag—" and slips onto the floor, making a rough noise like a seal.

Paul screams. There's more of the *ag-ag* business and more gruesome convulsive disintegrations, until by two in the morning Delphi is nothing but a warm little bundle of vegetative functions hitched to some expensive hardware—the same that sustained her before her life began. Joe has finally persuaded Paul to let him at the waldo-cabinet. Paul stays by her long enough to see her face change in a dreadfully alien and coldly convincing way, and then he stumbles out bleakly through the group in Tesla's office.

Behind him Joe is working wet-faced, sweating to reintegrate the fantastic complex of circulation, respiration, endocrines, midbrain homeostases, the patterned flux that was a human being—it's like saving an orchestra abandoned in midair. Joe is also crying a little; he alone had truly loved P. Burke. P. Burke, now a dead pile on a table, was the greatest cybersystem he has ever known and he never forgets her.

The end, really.

You're curious?

Sure, Delphi lives again. Next year she's back on the yacht getting sympathy for her tragic breakdown. But there's a different chick in Chile, because while Delphi's new operator is competent, you don't get two P. Burke's in a row—for which GTX is duly grateful.

The real belly-bomb of course is Paul. He was *young*, see. Fighting abstract wrong. Now life has clawed into him and he goes through gut rage and grief and grows in human wisdom and resolve. So much so that you won't be surprised, some time later, to find him—where?

In the GTX boardroom, dummy. Using the advantage of his birth to radicalize the system. You'd call it "boring from within."

That's how he put it, and his friends couldn't agree more. It gives them a warm, confident feeling to know that Paul is up there. Sometimes one of them who's still around runs into him and gets a big hello.

And the sharp-faced lad?

Oh, he matures too. He learns fast, believe it. For instance, he's the first to learn that an obscure GTX research unit is actually getting something with their loopy temporal anomalizer project. True, he doesn't have a physics background, and he's bugged quite a few people. But he doesn't really learn about that until the day he stands where somebody points him during a test run—

—and wakes up lying on a newspaper headlined NIXON UNVEILS PHASE TWO.

Lucky he's a fast learner.

Believe it, zombie. When I say growth I mean *growth*. Capital appreciation. You can stop sweating. There's a great future there.

As a special bonus, Tor is pleased to present an excerpt from Swordspoint, *the remarkable novel by Ellen Kushner, coming in paperback from Tor in July.*

"*Swordspoint* is a scintillating gem. It's wicked, fascinating, beautifully written—and unique."
—Joan D. Vinge

"An elegant, talented, and vastly enjoyable novel."
—Samuel R. Delany

SWORDSPOINT

† † †

Chapter 1

Snow was falling on Riverside, great white feather-puffs that veiled the cracks in the façades of its ruined houses, slowly softening the harsh contours of jagged roof and fallen beam. Eaves were rounded with snow, overlapping, embracing, sliding into each other, capping houses all clustered together like a fairy-tale village. Little slopes of snow nestled in the slats of shutters still cosily latched against the night. It dusted the tops of fantastical chimneys that spiralled up from frosted roofs, and it formed white peaks in the ridges of the old coats of arms carved above the doorways. Only here and there a window, its glass long shattered, gaped like a black mouth with broken teeth, sucking snow into its maw.

Let the fairy-tale begin on a winter's morning, then, with one drop of blood new-fallen on the ivory snow: a drop as bright as a clear-cut ruby, red as the single spot of claret on the lace cuff. And it therefore follows that evil lurks behind each broken window, scheming malice and enchantment; while behind the latched shutters the good are sleeping their just sleeps at this early hour in Riverside. Soon they will arise to go about their business; and one, maybe, will be as lovely as the day, armed, as are the good, for a predestined triumph. . . .

But there is no one behind the broken windows; only eddies of snow drift across bare floorboards. The owners of the coats of arms have long since abandoned all claims to the houses they crest, and moved up to the Hill where they can look down on all the city. No king rules them any more, for good or ill. From the Hill, Riverside is a tiny splotch between two riverbanks, an unsavoury quarter in a prosperous city. The people who live there now like to think of themselves as evil, but they're really no worse than anyone else. And already this morning more than one drop of blood has been shed.

The blood lies on the snow of a formal winter garden, now trampled and muddy. A man lies dead, the snow filling in the hollows of his eyes, while another man is twisted up, grunting, sweating frog-ponds on the frozen earth, waiting for someone to come and help him. The hero of this little tableau has just vaulted the garden wall and is running like mad into the darkness while the darkness lasts.

The falling snow made it hard for him to see. The fight hadn't badly winded him, but he was hot and sweaty, and he could feel his heart pounding in his chest. He ignored it, making for Riverside, where no one was likely to follow him.

He could have stayed, if he'd wanted to. The swordfight had been very impressive, and the party guests had been well entertained. The winter garden party and its outcome would be talked about for weeks. But if he stayed, the swordsman knew that he would be offered wine, and rich pastry, and asked boring questions about his technique, and difficult questions about who had arranged the fight. He ran on.

Under his cloak, his shirt was spattered with blood, and the Watch would want to know what he was doing up on the Hill at this hour. It was their right to know; but his profession forbade him to answer, so he dodged around corners and caught his breath in doorways until he'd left the splendours of the Hill behind, working his way down through the city. It was breaking dawn when he came to the river, flowing murky green under the Bridge. No one waited there to challenge him, so he set his foot on the stone, ploughing through snowdrifts and the messy trails of other late-night workers who'd come before him, until he'd put the river safely between himself and the rest of the city. He stood now in Riverside, where the Watch never dared to come. People knew him here, and wouldn't bother him.

But when he opened the door to his landlady's, there was a considerable crowd assembled, all wanting to know about the fight.

Other Riversiders had been on the Hill too, that night, burgling houses and collecting gossip, and already the rumours had begun. The swordsman answered their questions with as much civility as he could muster, suddenly awash with exhaustion. He gave Marie his shirt to wash, and climbed the stairs to his own rooms.

Less than an hour earlier, Marie the whore and laundress, who also rented out rooms by the week, had lain snoring lightly in the arms of a dear client, unaware of the impending excitement. Her friend was a sailor turned coiner, whose wooden leg leaned handily against the headboard. He was her fifth and last of the night, and she, not as young as she once was, slept through the initial pounding on her shutters. The sailor stirred uneasily, dreaming of storms. When the knock came harder, Marie bolted up with a cry, then shrieked at the cold outside the blanket.

'Marie! Marie!' The voice through the shutter was muffled but insistent. 'Open up and tell us all about it!'

Marie sighed. It must be St Vier again: every time the swordsman got up to something they came to her to find out the details. This time, it was annoying to admit, she didn't know—but then, she didn't have to tell *them* that. With the laugh that had always made her popular, Marie got up and unbolted the door to the house.

Her sailor huddled in a corner of the bed while her friends trooped in, taking over the room with the ease of familiarity. It was the right room for socialising, having been the front parlour when the house was a noble's town house. The cherubs painted on the ceiling were flecked with mould; but most of the laurel-leaf moulding still framed the walls, and the fireplace was real marble. Marie's friends spread their wet cloaks out on the gilded escritoire, now missing all its drawers, and over the turquoise velvet chair no one could sit on because of the uncertainty of its legs. Lightfinger Lucie coaxed the fire to a blaze, and Sam Bonner produced a jug of something that made the sailor feel much better.

'You know,' said Sam ponderously, 'your St Vier's gone and killed a duke this time.'

Sam Bonner was a former pickpocket with an unhandy taste for the bottle. He'd been repeating the same thing for half an hour now, and his friends were getting tired of correcting him. 'Not the *duke*, Sam,' one of them tried again. 'He's *working* for the duke. He killed two *swordsmen*, see, in the duke's garden.'

'No, no, in Lord Horn's garden. *Three* swordsmen, I heard,' another asserted, 'and from a very reliable source. Two dead, one wounded, and I'm taking odds on whether he'll live till morning!'

'Done!'

Marie sat on the bed with the blankets wrapped around her feet, letting the betting and the squabbling swirl around her. 'Who's dead?—Lynch—de Maris—Not a scratch on him—Horn's garden—Hired St Vier?—Not

St Vier, Lynch—Wounded—Dying—Who's paying St Vier?—Horn—the duke—the devil— How much?—More'n *you'll* ever see—'

More people trickled in, adding to the clamour. 'St Vier's been killed—captured— Five to one—'

They barely noticed when another man came in and silently took a place just inside the door. Sam Bonner was roaring, 'Well, *I* say he's the best dam' swordsman in the whole dam' city! No, I'm lying—in the world!'

The young man by the doorway smiled, and said, 'Excuse me. Marie?'

He was younger than most of them there; dark-haired, of average height, his face dirty and stubbled.

'Who the hell is that?' Sam Bonner growled.

'The best dam' swordsman in the world,' Lightfinger Lucie answered with pardonable malice.

'I'm sorry to bother you,' the swordsman said to Marie, 'but you know how the stains set.' He took off his cloak, revealing a white shirt ugly with blood. He pulled the shirt over his head, and tossed it into a corner. For a moment the iron tang of blood cut through the smells of whisky and wet wool. 'I can pay you next week,' he said. 'I made some money.'

'Oh, that's fine with me,' Marie said with off-handed airiness, showing off.

He turned to go, but they stopped him with the shouting of his name: 'St Vier!'

'St Vier! Who's dead, then?'

'De Maris,' he answered curtly. 'And maybe Lynch, by now. Excuse me, please.'

No one reached out a hand to stop him as he walked through the door.

The smell of frying fish made the swordsman's stomach lurch. It was his young gentleman, the University student, wrapped in his scholar's robe, hovering like a black bat over the frying pan in the ornamented fireplace.

'Good morning,' St Vier said. 'You're up early.'

'I'm always up early, Richard.' The student didn't turn around. 'You're the one who stays out all night killing people.' His voice was its usual cool drawl, taunting in its nonchalance. The accent, with its crisp consonants and long vowels, took Richard back to the Hill: for a moment he was once again crouched amid the topiary of the pleasure garden, hearing the same tones ringing on the air from the party guests. 'Who was the poor soul this time?'

'Just a couple of swordsmen. It was supposed to be a duel with Hal Lynch, I thought I told you. Our patrons set it up to take place at this crazy garden party of Lord Horn's. Can you imagine, having a party outdoors in this weather?'

'They would have had furs. And admired the landscaping.'

'I suppose.' While he spoke, the swordsman was cleaning his sword. It was a light, flexible duelling weapon of a sort only he, with his reputation and his reflexes, could carry around Riverside with authority. 'Anyway, Lynch got started, and then de Maris popped out of the shrubbery and started coming at me.'

'Whatever for?'

Richard sighed. 'Who knows? He's Horn's house swordsman; maybe he thought I was attacking his master. Anyway, Lynch stepped aside, and I killed de Maris. He was out of practice,' he added, polishing the blade with a soft cloth. 'Lynch was good enough, he always has been. But our patrons wanted it past first blood, so I think I killed him. I *think* . . .' He scowled. 'It was a clumsy stroke. I slipped on some old ice.'

The young man poked at the fish. 'Do you want some?'

'No, thanks. I'm just going to bed.'

'Well, it's revolting cold,' the scholar said with satisfaction, 'I shall have to eat it all myself.'

'Do that.'

St Vier passed into the adjoining room, which contained a clothes chest that also held his swords, wrapped in oil cloth, and a large, heavily carved bed. He had bought the bed the last time he had any money; seen it in a Riverside market stall full of odds-and-ends retrieved from the old houses, and fallen in love with it.

He looked at the bed. It did not appear to have been slept in. Curious, he returned to the front room.

'How was your night?' he asked. He noticed the pair of wet boots standing in the corner.

'Fine,' the scholar answered, daintily picking bones out of his fish. 'I thought you said you were tired.'

'Alec,' said Richard, 'It really isn't safe for you to be going out alone here after dark. People get wild, and not everyone knows who you are yet.'

'No one knows who I am.' Alec dreamily laced his long fingers in his hair. His hair was fine and leaf-brown, worn down his back in the long tail that was the defiant emblem of University scholars. He had been in Riverside since autumn, and his clothes and his accent were the only signs of where he had come from. 'Look.' Alec's eyes, turned to the window, were dark and green, like the water under the Bridge. 'It's still snowing. You can die in the snow. You're cold, but it doesn't hurt. They say you get warmer and warmer, and then you fall asleep. . . .'

'We can go out later. If anyone is trying to kill you, I'd better know about it.'

'Why?'

'I can't let them,' the swordsman said; 'it would ruin my reputation.' He yawned. 'I hope at least you had your knife with you.'

'I lost it.'

'Again? Well, never mind. I can get you another when the money for the fight comes in.' St Vier shook out his arms, and flexed them against the wall. 'If I don't go to sleep soon, I'm going to start waking up, and then I'll feel rotten for the rest of the day. 'Night, Alec.'

'Good night, Richard.' The voice was low and amused; of course, it was morning. But he was much too tired to care. He placed his sword within reach of the bed, as he always did. As he drifted off, he seemed to see a series of white images, scenes carved in snow. Frosty gardens, their branches lush with white roses and crystal thorns; ladies with floating spun-sugar hair escorted by ivory gallants; and, for himself, opponents with long bright swords of clear and gleaming ice.

Chapter 2

By midday, most of the nobles on the Hill could be counted on to be awake. The Hill sat lordly above the rest of the city, honey-combed with mansions, landscaped lawns, elaborate gates and private docks on the cleanest part of the river. Its streets had been built expressly wide and smooth enough to accommodate the carriages of nobles, shortly after carriages had been invented. Usually, mornings on the Hill were passed in leisurely exchange of notes written on col-oured, scented and folded paper, read and composed in various states of dishabille over cups of rich chocolate and crisp little trian-gles of toast (all the nourishment that ought to be managed after a night's revelling); but on the morning after the garden duel, with the night's events ripe for comment, no one had the patience to wait for a reply, so the streets were unusually crowded with car-riages and pedestrians of rank.

The Duke of Karleigh was gone from the

city. From what anyone could discover, the duke had left Lord Horn's party not an hour after the fight, gone home, ordered up his carriage despite the snow, and departed before dawn for his estates in the south without a word to anyone. The first swordsman who had fought St Vier, a man named Lynch, had died at around 10 that morning, so there was no asking him whether Karleigh had hired him for the duel, although the duke's abrupt departure upon Lynch's defeat seemed to confirm that he had. St Vier had disappeared back into Riverside, but whoever had hired him was expected to step forward momentarily to claim the stylish and elegant victory over Karleigh. So far, no one had.

Meanwhile, Lord Horn was certainly making enough of a fuss over the use his gardens had been put to, never mind the loss of his house swordsman, the impetuous de Maris; but that, as Lady Halliday remarked to the Duchess Tremontaine, meant precisely what it was supposed to mean. Horn was doubtless trying to coast on the notoriety that the event had given his otherwise unremarkable party for as long as possible. Both ladies had been there, along with most of the city's great aristocracy, many of whom Karleigh was known to have quarrelled with at one time or another.

'At least,' said the Duchess, tilting her elegant head, 'it seems to have rid us of my lord of Karleigh for the rest of the winter. I cannot commend his mysterious opponent too heartily for that service. Odious man. Do you know, Mary, how he insulted me last year? Well, it's just as well you don't; but I assure you I shall never forget it.'

Mary, Lady Halliday, smiled at her companion. The two women were seated in the sunny morning room of the Halliday townhouse, drinking tiny cups of bitter chocolate. Both were clothed in billowing yards of soft, exquisite lace, giving them the look of two goddesses rising from the foam. Their heads, one brown and one silver-fair, were perfectly coiffed, their eyebrows finely plucked. The tips of their fingers, round and smooth, peeped continually through the lace like little pink shells.

'So,' the duchess concluded, 'it's no wonder someone finally got vexed enough to set St Vier on him.'

'Not *on him*, precisely,' Mary Halliday amended. 'The duke was, after all, warned in time to find himself another swordsman to take the challenge.'

'Pity,' the duchess growled.

Lady Halliday poured out more chocolate, musing, 'I wonder what it was all about. If it had been anything clever or amusing, the quarrel would not be kept such a secret—like poor Lynch's last duel, when Lord Godwin's eldest hired him to fight Monteith's champion over whose mistress was prettier. That was nice; but then, it wasn't to the death.'

'Duels are to the death only when one of two things is at stake: power or money.'

'What about honour?'

'What do you think honour buys?' the duchess asked cynically.

Lady Halliday was a quiet, shy young woman with none of her friend's fashionable talent for clever chatter. Her voice was generally low, her speech soft—just what men always claimed to want in a woman, but were never actually drawn to in the drawing room. However, her marriage to the widowed Basil, Lord Halliday, a popular city aristocrat, was said to have been a love match, so society was prepared to credit her with hidden depths. She was, in fact, by no means stupid, and if she answered the duchess with ponderous slowness it was only that she was, as was her habit, weighing her words against the thoughts behind them. 'I think that *honour* is used to mean so many different things that no one can be sure of what it really is. Certainly young Monteith claimed his honour to be satisfied when Lynch won the fight, while privately Basil told me he thought the whole thing a pointless exercise in scandal.'

'That is because young Monteith is an idiot, and your husband is a sensible man,' the duchess said firmly. 'I imagine Lord Halliday is much more pleased with this fight of Karleigh's; at least it accomplished something practical.'

'More than that,' said Lady Halliday. Her voice had dropped, and she leaned out a little over the furbelows of lace toward her friend. 'He is immensely pleased that Karleigh has left town. You know the Council of

Lords elects its head again this spring. Basil wishes to be re-elected.'

'And quite rightly,' Diane said stoutly. 'He is the best Crescent Chancellor the city has had in decades—the best, some say, since the fall of the monarchy, which is generous praise indeed. Surely he expects no difficulty in being re-elected?'

'You are kind. Of course the city loves him . . . but . . .' She leaned even closer, her porcelain cup held out of harm's way. 'I must tell you. In fact there is a great deal of difficulty. My lord—Basil—has held the Crescent for three consecutive terms now. But it seems there's a law that no one may hold it for four straight terms.'

'Is there?' said the duchess vaguely. 'What a shame. Well, I'm sure that won't matter to anyone.'

'My lord is hoping to put it to the vote in spring. The entire Council may choose to override the law in the case. But the Duke of Karleigh has been quietly approaching people all winter, reminding them of it, spreading all sorts of nonsense on the danger of too much power in the hands of one nobleman. As though my lord would take that power— as though he *could*, when he expends all his strength just keeping the state together!' Lady Halliday's cup rattled on its saucer; she steadied it and said, 'You may see why my lord is pleased that Karleigh's gone, if only for a month or two.'

'Yes,' the duchess said softly; 'I thought he might be.'

'But Diane—' Suddenly Lady Halliday

seized her hand in an eloquent hissing of lace. 'It may not be enough. I am so concerned. He *must* keep the Crescent, he is just beginning to accomplish what he set out to do; to lose it now, even for a term, would be a terrible set-back for him and for the city. You hold Tremontaine in your own right, you could vote in Council if you chose. . . . '

'Now, Mary . . .' Smiling, the duchess disengaged her hand. 'You know I never meddle in politics. The late duke would not have wished it.'

Whatever further entreaty Lady Halliday might have made was forestalled by the announcement of two more guests, the Godwins, who were shown up with the greatest dispatch.

It was unusual for Lady Godwin to be in town in winter; she was fond of the country and, being past that time of life when social duties required her presence in the city, spent most of her time with her husband overseeing the Godwins' great house and estates at Amberleigh. The responsibility of representing the family's interests in the city and on the Council of Lords fell to Lord Godwin's heir, his only son Michael. Lord Michael's name was surrounded with the pleasing aura of scandal appropriate to a young noble who did not need to be too careful of what was said about him. He was an exceptionally attractive young man, and knew it. His liaisons were many, but always in good taste; they might be said to be his distinguishing social excess, as he eschewed those of gambling, quarrelling and dress.

Now he escorted his mother into the room, every inch the well-groomed, dutiful son. He had attended parties given by the duchess and by the Hallidays, but was not well enough acquainted himself with either lady to have visited her privately.

His mother was greeting her friends with kisses, all three women using each other's first names. He followed her with a proper bow and kiss of the hand, murmuring their titles. Diane of Tremontaine said over his bent head, 'How charming to find a young man willing to call upon ladies at a decent hour and in conventional fashion.'

'Barely decent,' Mary Halliday amended, 'with us still in our morning clothes.'

'They are so lovely, you ought never change them,' Lydia Godwin was saying to her; and to Diane, 'Of course: he was very well brought up—and the city hasn't altered his breeding, whatever his father might say. I can trust you, can't I, Michael?'

'Of course, madam.' Automatically he answered the tone of her voice. He had heard nothing since the duchess's comment, acid and piquant. He was surprised that a woman of her stature knew enough about his adventures to be able to make such a pointed remark, and was impressed with her audacity in making it in front of the others. The women were talking now, of the season, of his father's grain estates, as he swept his long-lashed gaze over her. She was beautiful, delicate and fair, with the true aristocrat's fragility that all fashionable city ladies strove to affect. He knew she must be closer to his mother's age than to his own. His mother had allowed herself to run to plumpness. It made her look comfortable; this lady looked entrancing. Suddenly Diane was meeting his look. She held it for a moment, unperturbed, before turning back to his mother and saying, 'And now, no doubt, you are disgusted with yourself for having missed Horn's winter ball! I nearly had a headache myself at the last minute, but I'd already had the dress made, and where else is one going to wear white at this time of year? Poor Horn! I've heard that someone is saying that it was he himself who hired *both* swordsmen, just to entertain his guests!'

'Not a very kind "someone",' put in Lord Michael, 'considering how his house swordsman teamed up with Master Lynch against St Vier—'

'Who still contrived to win!' his mother interrupted. 'I do wish I'd seen it. I hear it's harder and harder to hire St Vier to fight for anyone.' She sighed. 'Swordsmen are getting so above themselves these days, from what I hear. When I first came to the city, I remember, there was a man named Stirling—one of the richest men on Teviot Street, with a big house and gardens—*he* was a swordsman, one of the greats, and he was paid accordingly. But no one had to *ask* him who he felt like fighting that particular day; you just sent him the money and he did the job.'

'Mother,' Michael teased her. 'I never knew you had such a passion for swordplay! Shall I hire you St Vier for your birthday?'

'Now, who will he fight at Amberleigh?

Don't be silly, my darling,' she said fondly, patting his hand.

'Besides,' Lady Halliday said, 'chances are good that he doesn't *do* birthdays.' Her friends looked startled at this pronouncement, coming from her. 'Well, you've heard the story haven't you? About Lord Montague and his daughter's wedding?' To her dismay they said they hadn't, and she was obliged to begin: 'She was his only daughter, you see, so he didn't mind the expense, he wanted to hire the best swordsman there was to take the part of the guard at the altar . . . It was only last summer, you *must* have . . . Oh, well—St Vier had fought for Montague before, so he had the man up to his house— well, in his study, I imagine—to ask him properly, so no one would think there was anything shady going on—you know all you need before a wedding's people getting jumpy over swords—so Montague offered him the job, purely ceremonial, he wouldn't even have to *do* anything. And St Vier looked at him, pleasantly enough, Montague told us, and said, "Thank you, but I don't do weddings anymore." '

Lady Godwin shook her head. 'Imagine. Stirling did weddings; he did Julia Hetley's, I remember it. I wanted him to do mine, but he was dead then. I forget who we got instead.'

'My lady,' said Michael, with that impish grin she had always found irresistible, 'shall I take up the sword to please you? I could add to the family fortunes.'

'As though they needed adding to,' the

duchess said drily. 'I suppose you could save yourself the expense of hiring a swordsman to fight your inevitable romantic quarrels, my lord. But aren't you a little old to be able to take it up successfully?'

'*Diane!*' his mother gurgled. This once he was grateful for her quick intercession. He was fighting back a blush, one of the drawbacks of his fair complexion. The lady was too personal, she presumed upon acquaintance with his mother to mock him . . . He was not used to women who did not care to please him. 'Michael, you are a perfect goose even to think of such a thing, and, Diane, you must not encourage him to quarrel, I'm sure his friends are bad enough. Oh, yes, no doubt Lord Godwin would be delighted to hear of his heir taking up the sword like any common street brawler. We saw to it that you had all the training you needed when you were a boy. You carry a petty-sword nicely, you can dance without catching your legs in it, and that should be enough for any gentleman.'

'There's Lord Arlen,' Lady Halliday said. 'You can't say *he's* not a gentleman.'

'Arlen is an eccentric,' Lady Godwin said firmly, 'and notably old-fashioned. I'm sure no young man of Michael's set would even consider such a thing.'

'Surely not, Lydia,' the exquisite duchess was saying consolingly. 'And Lord Michael a man of such style, too.' To his surprise she smiled at him, warmly and directly. 'There are men I know who would go to any lengths to annoy their parents. How fortunate you are, Lydia, in having a son you may trust always to do you credit. I am sure he could never be any more serious about taking up the sword than something equally ridiculous . . . University, for instance.'

The talk turned to notorious sons, effectively shutting Michael out from contributing to it. Another time he might have listened avidly and with some amusement as they discussed various of his friends and acquaintances, so that he could store up anecdotes to repeat at card parties. But although no trace of it showed in his pleasant bearing and handsome face, Lord Michael was feeling increasingly sullen, and wondering how he might possibly leave without offending his mother, whom he had promised to accompany on all her calls that day. The company of women, making no effort to include him, made him feel, not so much as if he were a child again—for he had been a very fetching child, and adults had always stopped to notice him—but as though he had wandered into a cluster of foreigners, all chattering with animation in another language; or as though he were a ghost in the room, or a piece of useless and uninteresting furniture. Even the alluring duchess, though clearly not unaware of his interest, failed to be entirely concerned with him. At present, for example, she seemed to be much more taken with a series of stories his mother was telling about one of his lunatic cousins. Perhaps he might see her again soon, in better circumstances—only to renew the acquaintance, of course; his current lover's possessiveness he found exciting, and was not yet ready to give up.

Finally, they returned to the more interesting question of whether Lord Horn had had anything to do with the fighting in his gardens. Michael was able to say sagely, 'Well, I hope the suggestion will not get back to Horn's ears. He's liable to become offended and hire himself another swordsman to take care of the rumour-mongers.'

The duchess's fine eyebrows rose in twin arcs. 'Oh? Are you intimately acquainted with the gentleman and his habits?'

'No, madam,' he answered, covering his discomfort at her challenge with a show of surprise. 'But I know him to *be* a gentleman; I do not think he would readily brook the suggestion that he had intentionally set two swordsmen against one, whether in private quarrel or to please his guests.'

'Well, you're probably right there,' she conceded; 'whether he actually did so or not. Horn has been so careful of his reputation these last few years—he'd probably deny stealing honey if his fingers were caught in the jar. He was much more agreeable when he still had something to occupy his time.'

'Surely he is as busy now as any nobleman?' Lady Halliday asked, sure she was missing some vital connection. Lydia Godwin said nothing, but scowled at her knuckles.

'Of course,' Diane said generously, 'you were not yet come to the city then, Mary. Dear, how gossip will trip us up! You will not know that some years past Lord Horn was the reigning beauty. He managed to capture the eyes of Lord Galing, God rest him, who was at the time gaining power in the Council, but didn't quite know what to do with it all. Horn told him. They were a strong combination for a while, Horn with his ambition, and Galing with his talent. I feared—along with my husband, of course—that Galing would be made Chancellor. But Galing died, not a moment too soon, and Horn's influence has faded. I'm sure it galls him. It's probably why he insists on giving such showy parties. His star has definitely fallen: he lacks the coin for further extravagant purchases. Not, of course, that Lord Halliday would wish for any distracting influence!'

Mary Halliday smiled prettily, her colour reflecting the rose ribbons on her cap. Lady Godwin looked up and said a trifle brusquely, 'Why is it, Diane, that you seem to know the single most unpleasant story about everyone in the city?'

'I suppose,' she answered blithely, 'because there are so many unpleasant people. How right you are to stay at Amberleigh, my dear.'

In despair Michael thought: If they start on about the family again, I shall fall off my chair. He said, 'I've been thinking, actually, about Karleigh.' The duchess favoured him with her attention. Her eyes were the frosty silver of winter clouds. He felt a delicate shiver as they brushed over him.

'You are quite sure, then,' she said, in a low, melodious voice, 'that it was the duke who hired Lynch?' It was as though she had said something quite different, for his ears alone. His lips were lightly parted; and at last he saw, looking at her, his own beauty reflected there. But before he could answer, his mother cried, 'Of course it was Karleigh! Why else would he leave town first thing this morning, making no excuses to anyone—unless he left a note for Horn apologising for the use his garden was put to . . .'

'Not his style,' observed the duchess.

'Then it is clear,' Lady Godwin said triumphantly, 'that he *had* to get out of the city. His man lost the fight! And St Vier may still be in the pay of his opponent. If Karleigh stayed, he might have to keep hiring other swordsmen to go up against St Vier, until he ran out of money, or talent. And then he'd be up against St Vier himself—and then, you know, he'd surely be dead. The duke doesn't know any more of swordplay than Michael, I'm sure.'

'But I am sure,' the duchess said, again with that strange double-edged tone, 'that Lord Michael would know what to do with it if he did.'

Something fluttered at the base of his spine. Resolutely he took control of the conversation. He turned directly to the duchess, speaking assertively, summoning all the confidence of a man used to having his opinions heeded. 'As a matter of fact, madam, I am *not* sure that the Duke of Karleigh hired Lynch. I was wondering whether it were not just as likely that he had hired St Vier instead.'

'Oh, Michael,' said his mother impatiently. 'Then why would Karleigh have left town when his man *won*?'

'Because he was still afraid of the person who did hire Lynch.'

'Interesting,' said the duchess. Her silvery eyes seemed to grow bigger, like a cat's. 'And not altogether impossible. Your son, Lydia, would seem to have a far more complex grasp of the situation than any of us.'

Her eyes had turned from him, and the mocking disdain was back in her voice. But he had had her for a moment—had her interest, had her seeing him entirely. He wondered what he had done to lose her.

The door to the morning room opened, and a tall, broad-framed man came in unannounced. A sense of exertion and the outdoors hung about him: his dark hair was ruffled all over his head, and his handsome face was high-coloured by the wind. Unlike Michael, with his tight-fitting, pastel costume, this man wore loose, dark clothes, with mud-splashed boots up to his thighs.

Mary Halliday's face transformed with brightness when she saw him. Being a good hostess and a well-mannered woman, she stayed seated amongst her guests; but her bright eyes never left her husband.

Basil, Lord Halliday, Crescent Chancellor of the Council of Lords, bowed to his wife's company, a smile creasing his weathered face.

She spoke to him formally. 'My lord! We did not expect you back so soon as this.'

His smile deepened with mischief and affection. 'I know,' he answered, coming to kiss both her hands. 'I came home directly, before even going to report to Ferris. I should have remembered that you'd have company.'

'Company is delighted to see you,' said the Duchess Tremontaine, 'although I'm sure Lady Halliday is more so. She wouldn't admit it, but I believe the thought of you riding out to Helmsleigh alone to face a cordon of rebellious weavers unsettled her equilibrium.'

Halliday laughed. 'I was hardly alone. I took a troop of City Guard with me to impress them.'

His wife caught his eyes, asking seriously, 'How did it go?'

'Well enough,' he answered her. 'They have some legitimate complaints. Foreign wool has been driving prices down, and the new tax is hard on the smaller communes. I'll have to take it up with my lord Ferris. I'll tell you all about it, but not till afterward, or the Dragon Chancellor will be annoyed for not having been the first to hear.'

Lady Halliday frowned. 'I still think Ferris should have gone instead. The Exchequer is his concern.'

He sent her a brief glance of warning before saying lightly, 'Not at all! What is a mere Dragon Chancellor when compared with the head of the entire Council of Lords? This way they were flattered, and felt that enough attention was being paid to them. Now, when I send Chris Nevilleson out to take a full report, they'll be nice to him. I think the matter should be settled soon.'

'Well, I should think so!' said Lady Godwin. 'Imagine some pack of weavers raising their shuttles against a Council order.'

Michael laughed, thinking of his friend riding out to Helmsleigh on one of his fine horses. 'Poor Chris! Why do you assign him all the most unpleasant tasks, my lord?'

'He volunteers. I believe he wishes to be of service.'

'He adores you, Basil,' Lady Halliday said brightly. Michael Godwin raised his eyebrows, and the colour rushed into her face. 'Oh, no! I mean . . . he admires Lord Halliday . . . his work . . .'

'Anyone would,' said the duchess comfortably. 'I adore him myself. And if I wished to advance to any political power, I should most certainly station myself at his side.' Her friend smiled gratefully at her over the rim of the chocolate cup behind which she had taken refuge. And Michael felt, in consternation, that he had just been measured and found wanting. 'In fact,' the duchess continued blithely, 'I have been grieving over how seldom I see him—or any of you—when not surrounded by other admirers. Let us all dine together privately a few weeks from today. You have heard of Steele's fireworks? He's sending them off over the river to celebrate his birthday. It promises to be quite a show. Of course I told him it was the wrong time of year, but he said he couldn't change his birthday to suit the weather, and he has always been uncommonly fond of fireworks. They will entertain the populace, and give the rest of us something to do. So we're all to dust off our summer barges and go out on the river and enjoy ourselves. Mine will certainly hold us all, and I believe my cook can put together a tolerable picnic; if we all dress up warmly it won't be so bad.' She turned her charming smile on Basil Halliday. 'I shall invite Lord Ferris, my lord, only if you two promise not to spend the whole evening talking politics. . . . and Chris Nevilleson and his sister, I think. Perhaps I had better include a few other young men, to ensure that Lord Michael has someone to talk to.'

Michael's flush of embarrassment lasted through the chatter of thanks. He was able to cover it by straightening his hose. A fall of lace cuff brushed his cheek as the duchess stood by his mother saying, 'Oh, Lydia, what a shame, to have to leave town so soon! I hope Lord Michael will be able to represent you at my picnic?' He stopped before he could begin to stammer something out, and simply rose and offered her his seat by his mother. She sank into it with a willow's grace, and looked up at him, smiling. 'You will come, will you not, my lord?'

Michael squared his shoulders, sharply aware of the close fit of his jacket, the hang of his sleeves. Her offered hand lay on his like a featherweight, soft, white and elusively perfumed. He was careful only to brush it with his lips. 'Your servant, madam,' he murmured, looking straight up into her eyes.

'Such manners.' The duchess returned the look. 'What a delightful young man. I shall expect you, then.'

Chapter 3

Richard St Vier, the swordsman, awoke later that day, in the middle of the afternoon. The house was quiet and the room was cold. He got up and dressed quickly, not bothering to light the bedroom fire.

He stepped softly into the other room, knowing which floorboards were likely to creak. He saw the top of Alec's head, nestled into a burlap-covered chaise longue he was fond of because it had griffins' heads carved into the armrests. Alec had built up the fire and drawn the chair up close to it. Richard thought Alec might be asleep; but then he saw Alec's shoulder shift and heard the crackle of paper as he turned the pages of a book.

Richard limbered up against the wall for awhile, then took up a blunt-tipped practice sword and began to attack the chipped plaster wall with it, striking up and down an imaginary line with steady, rhythmic precision. There was a counterattack from the other side of the wall: three blows from a heavy fist caused their remaining flakes of paint to tremble.

'*Will you shut that racket up?*' a voice demanded through the wall.

Richard put his sword down in disgust. 'Hell,' he said, 'they're home.'

'Why don't you kill them?' the man in the chair asked lazily.

'What for? Marie'd only replace them with some more. She needs the rent money. At least this bunch doesn't have babies.'

'True.' One long leg and then another swung out from the chaise to plant themselves on the floor. 'It's mid-afternoon. The snow has stopped. Let's go out.'

Richard looked at him. 'Anywhere special?'

'The Old Market,' said Alec, 'might be entertaining. If you're still in the mood, after those other two.'

Richard got a heavier sword, and buckled it on. Alec's ideas of 'entertaining' were violent. His blood began to race, not unpleasantly. People had learned not to bother him; now they must learn the same about Alec. He followed him into the winter air, which was cold and sharp like a hunting morning.

The streets of Riverside were mostly deserted at this time of day, and a thick snow-cover muffled what sounds there were. The oldest houses were built so close together that their eaves almost touched across the street, eaves elaborately carved, throwing shadows onto the last flakes of painted coats of arms on the walls below them. No modern carriage could pass between the houses of Riverside; its people walked, and hid in the twisting byways, and the Watch never followed them there. The nobles drove their well-sprung carriages along the broad, sunlit avenues of the upper city, leaving their ancestors' houses to whomever chose to occupy them. Most would be surprised to know how many still held deeds to Riverside houses; and few would be eager to collect the rent.

Alec sniffed the air. 'Bread. Someone's baking bread.'

'Are you hungry?'

'I'm always hungry.' The young man pulled his scholar's robe tighter around him. Alec was tall, and a little too thin, with none of the swordsman's well-sprung grace. With the layers of clothes he had piled on underneath the robe, he looked like a badly wrapped package. 'Hungry and cold. It's what I came to Riverside for. I got tired of the luxurious splendour of University life. The magnificent meals, the roaring fires in the comfy lecture halls. . . .' A gust of wind whipped powdered snow off a roof and into their faces. Alec cursed with a student's elaborate fluency. 'What a stupid place to live! No wonder anyone with any sense left here long ago. The streets are a perfect wind-tunnel between the two rivers. It's like asking to be put in cold-storage. . . . I hope they're paying you soon for that idiotic duel, because we're almost out of wood and my fingers are turning blue as it is.'

'They're paying me,' Richard answered

comfortably. 'I can pick up the money to-morrow, and buy wood on the way home.' Alec had been complaining of the cold since the first ground-frost. He kept their rooms hotter than Richard ever had, and still shivered and wrapped himself in blankets all day. Whatever part of the country he came from, it was probably not the northern mountains, and not the house of a poor man. All evidence so far of Alec's past was circumstantial: things like the fire, and the accent, and his inability to fight, all spoke nobility. But at the same time he had no money, no known people or title, and the University gown hung on his slumped shoulders as though it belonged there. The University was for poor scholars, or clever men hoping to better themselves and acquire posts as secretaries or tutors to the nobility.

Richard said, 'Anyway, I thought you won lots of money off Rodge the other night, dicing.'

'I did.' Alec loosed one edge of his cloak to make sweeping gestures with his right hand. 'He won it back from me next night. In fact I owe him money; it's why we're not going to Rosalie's.'

'It's all right; he knows I'm good for it.'

'He cheats,' Alec said. 'They all cheat. I don't know how you can cheat with straight dice, but as soon as I find out I'm going to get rich off Rodge and all his smelly little friends.'

'Don't,' said Richard. 'That's for these types, not for you. You don't have to cheat, you're a gentleman.'

As soon as it was out he knew it had been the wrong thing to say. He could feel Alec's tension, almost taste the blue coldness of the air between them. But Alec only said, 'A gentleman, Richard? What nonsense. I'm just a poor student who was stupid enough to spend time with my books when I could have been out drinking and learning how to load dice.'

'Well,' St Vier said equably, 'you're certainly making up for it now.'

'Aren't I just.' Alec smiled with grim pleasure.

The Old Market wasn't old, nor was it properly a market. A square of once-elegant houses had been gutted at the ground floor, so that each house opened at the front. The effect was like a series of little boxed stage sets, each containing a fire and a group of Riversiders crowded around it, their hands stuffed under their armpits or held out to the fire, engaged in what could only loosely be termed marketing: a little dicing, a little flirting, drinking, and trying to sell each other stolen objects, shifting from foot to foot in the cold.

In front of one of them Alec suddenly stopped. 'Here,' he said. 'Let's go in here.'

There was nothing to distinguish this one from any of the others. Richard followed him to the fire. Alec's movements were languid, with a studied grace that the swordsman's eye recognised as the burden of feverish tension held in check. Other people noticed it too, though what they made of it was hard to say. Riverside was used to odd-looking people with odd moods. The woman nearest Alec moved nervously away, yielding her proximity to the fire. Across it a short man with a rag twisted around his sandy hair looked up from casting dice.

'Well, look who's here,' he said in a soft whine. 'Master Scholar.' A long gleam of metal slid from his side to his hand. 'I thought I told you last night I didn't want to see your face again.'

'Stupid face,' Alec corrected with airy condescension. 'You said you didn't want to see my *stupid* face *around* here again.' Someone giggled nervously. People had edged away from the dicer with the drawn sword. Without turning his head the man reached his free hand behind him and caught a small, pretty woman's wrist. He reeled her in to his side like a fish on a line, and held her there, fondling one breast. His eyes above her head dared anyone to react.

'That's good,' Alec said with lofty sarcasm. 'I used to know a man who could name any card you pulled from the deck without looking.'

'That's good.' The man mimicked his accent. 'Is that what they teach you at University, scholar, card tricks?'

The muscles tautened around Alec's mouth. 'They don't teach anyone anything at University. I had to learn to recognise people with duckshit for brains all by myself. But I think I'm pretty good at it, don't you?'

The girl squeaked when her captor's arm crushed her bosom. 'You're going to be gone,' he growled at Alec, 'by the time I count three.' Spit flecked the corner of his mouth.

Behind them the voices were murmuring, 'Six says he's gone by two ... by three ... Six says he stays. ...'

Alec stood where he was, his head cocked back, considering the other down the length of his nose. 'One,' the man counted. 'Two.'

'*Move*, you stupid clown!' someone cried. 'Brent'll kill you!'

'But I have to stay and help him,' Alec said with polite surprise. 'You can see he's stuck for the next one. It's "three," ' he told him kindly. 'The one after "two".'

Brent flung the girl aside. 'Draw,' he growled, 'if you've got a sword.'

The thin man in the scholar's robe raised his eyebrows. 'What if I haven't?'

'Well.' Brent came slowly around the fire with a swordsman's sure step. 'That would be a shame.'

He was halfway to the scholar when a by-stander spoke up. 'My fight,' he said clearly, so everyone heard.

Brent looked him over. Another swords-man. Harder to kill, but better for his repu-tation. 'Fine,' he purred in his insinuating whine. 'I'll take care of you first, and then finish off Mister Scholar, here.'

Richard slung his cloak around one arm. A woman near him looked at his face and gasped, 'St Vier!' Now the word was out; people were jostling to see; bets were chang-ing. Even as they pressed back to the walls to give the fighters room, the spectators were agitating; a few slipped out to fetch friends to watch the fight. Newcomers crowded across the open house-front.

Richard ignored them all. He was aware of Alec, safe to one side, his eyes wide and bright, his posture negligent.

'There's your third for today,' Alec said pleasantly. 'Kill him.'

Richard began as he usually did, running his opponent through some simple attacks, parrying the counterattack almost absently. It did give the other the chance to assess him as well, but usually that only served to unnerve them. Brent was quick, with a good swordsman's sixth sense for what was coming next; but his defence was seriously weaker on the left, poor fool. Enough practice on some good drills could have got him over that. Richard pretended he hadn't noticed, and played to his right. Aware that he was being tested, Brent tried to turn the fight so that he led the attack. Richard didn't let him. It flustered Brent; trying harder to gain control, he began to rush his counters, as though by coming in fast enough he could surprise St Vier into defence.

The swords were clashing rapidly now. It was the kind of fight spectators liked best: lots of relentless follow-through, without too much deliberation before each new series of moves. The woman Brent had been holding watched, cursing slowly and methodically under her breath, her fingers knotted together. Others were louder, calling encouragement, bets and enlightened commentary, filling each other in on the background of the fight.

Through his shield of concentration Richard heard the voices, though not the words they spoke. As the fight went on and he absorbed Brent's habits, he began to see not a personality but a set of obstructions to be removed. His fighting became less playful, more singleminded. It was the one thing knowledgeable spectators faulted him for: once he knew a man he seldom played him out in a show of technique, preferring to finish him off straightway.

Twice Richard passed up the chance to touch Brent's left arm. He wasn't interested in flesh wounds now. Other swordsmen might have made the cut for the advantage it would have given them; but the hallmark of St Vier's reputation was his ability to kill with one clean death wound. Brent knew he was fighting for his life. Even the onlookers were silent now, listening to the panting men's breath, the scrape of their boots and the clang of their swords. Over the heavy silence, Alec's voice drawled clearly, 'Didn't take long to scare *him*, did it? Told you I could spot them.'

Brent froze. Richard beat hard on his blade, to remind him of where he was. Brent's parry was fierce; he nearly touched St Vier's thigh countering, and Richard had to step back. His heel struck rock. He found he was backed against one of the stones surrounding the fire. He hadn't meant to lose that much ground; Alec had distracted him as well. He was already so hot he didn't feel the flames; but he was determined to preserve his boots. He dug in his back heel, and exchanged swordplay with Brent with his arm alone. He applied force, and nearly twisted the sword out of the other man's grasp. Brent paused, preparing another attack, watching him carefully for his. Richard came in blatantly low on the left, and when Brent moved to his defence St Vier came up over his arm and pierced his throat.

There was a flash of blue as the sword was pulled from the wound. Brent had stiffened bolt upright; now he toppled forward, his severed windpipe wheezing with gushing blood and air. Alec's face was pale, without expression. He looked down at the dying man long and hard, as though burning the sight into his eyes.

Amid the excitement of the fight's consummation, Richard stepped outside to clean his sword, whirling it swiftly in the air so that the blood flew off its surface and onto the snow.

One man came up to Alec. 'That was some fight,' he said friendlily. 'You rig it?'

'Yes.'

He indicated the swordsman outside. 'You going to tell me that young fellow's really St Vier?'

'Yes.'

Alec seemed numbed by the fight, the fever that had driven him sated by the death of his opponent, drugged now to a sluggish peace. But when St Vier came back in he spoke in his usual sardonic tones: 'Congratulations. I'll pay you when I'm rich.'

There was still one more thing to be done, and Richard did it. 'Never mind,' he said clearly, for those nearby to hear. 'They should know to leave you alone.'

He crossed to Alec by the fire, but a tiny woman, the one Brent had held, planted herself in front of him. Her eyes were red, her face pale and blotchy. She stared up at the swordsman and began to stutter furiously.

'What is it?' he asked.

'You owe me!' she exploded at last. 'Thhh-that man's ddd-dead and where'll I find another?'

'The same place you found him, I expect.'

'What'll I do for mm-money?'

Richard looked her up and down, from her painted eyes to gaudy stockings, and shrugged. She turned her shoulder in toward his chest and blinked up at him. 'I'm nice,' she squeaked. 'I'd work for you.'

Alec sneered at the little woman. 'I'd trip over you. We'd keep stepping on you in the dark.'

'Go away,' said Richard. 'I'm not a pimp.'

She stamped her small foot. 'You bastard! Riverside or no, I'll have the Watch on you!'

'You'd never go near the Watch,' said Richard, bored. 'They'd have you in the Chop before you could open your mouth.' He turned back to his friend. 'God, I'm thirsty. Let's go.'

They got as far as the doorway this time before Richard was stopped by another woman. She was a brilliant redhead of alarming prettiness, her paint expertly applied. Her cloak was of burgundy velvet, artfully draped to hide the worn spot. She placed her fingertips on Richard's arm, standing closer to him than he generally allowed. 'That was superb,' she said with throaty intimacy. 'I was so glad I caught the ending.'

'Thank you,' he replied courteously. 'I appreciate it.'

'Very good,' she pronounced. 'You gave him a fair chance, didn't keep him on the hook too long.'

'I've learned some good tricks by letting them show me what they can do first.'

She smiled warmly at him. 'You're no fool. You've got better every year. There's no stopping you from getting what you want. I could—'

'Excuse me,' Alec interrupted from the depths of boundless ennui, 'but who is this?'

The woman turned and swept him with her long lashes. 'I'm Ginnie Vandall,' she said huskily. 'And you?'

'My name is Alec.' He stared down at the tassels on her hem. 'Who pimps for you?'

The carmined lips pressed into a thin line, and the moment for a biting retort came and went. Knowing it was gone, she turned again to Richard, saying solicitously, 'My dear, you must be famished.'

He shrugged polite disavowal. 'Ginnie,' he asked her, 'is Hugo working now?'

She made a practised moue and looked into his eyes. 'Hugo is always working. He's gone so much I begin to wonder why I stay with him. They adore him on the Hill—too much, I sometimes think.'

'Nobody adores Richard,' Alec drawled. 'They're always trying to get him killed.'